THIS AIN'T NO VIDEO GAME, KID!

KEVIN STEVENS

Little Island

First published 2010
by Little Island
an imprint of New Island
2 Brookside
Dundrum Road
Dublin 14

www.littleisland.ie

ISBN 978-1-84840-947-7

British Library Cataloguing Data. A CIP catalogue record for this book is
available from the British Library.

Book design by Inka Hagen

Printed in Ireland by ColourBooks.

Little Island received financial assistance from
The Arts Council (An Chomhairle Ealaíon), Dublin, Ireland.

10 9 8 7 6 5 4 3 2 1

For my kids
Christian, Alice, Andrew
who like good books and cool games

ACKNOWLEDGEMENTS

My thanks to Siobhán Parkinson, who recognised that I had this book in me and helped bring it to life; to Elaina O'Neill, for her tactful and thorough copy-editing; and to my wife, Janice, for her unfailing encouragement and support.

1.

The plane was late, so Jack's dad was in a bad mood. He pretended he wasn't. He pretended, like he always did, that he was *in control*. But he was in a bad mood. Jack could tell and so could his mom.

They stared at the arrivals screen, crammed with information including a flashing green DELAYED beside the British Airways flight from London. 'They don't give you any information,' his dad said. 'Zip. They have no concept of customer service.'

'Not long now, Howard.'

His mom had a jar of phrases she reached into whenever his dad got like this. 'Just relax.' 'Keep your voice down.' 'Sure, what else would we be doing?' All delivered in the soft Irish accent she had never lost.

'We don't *know* how long, Clare. That's my point.'

Howard stalked off, looking goofy in his Mariners baseball cap and powder-blue polo shirt and those chino shorts that were basically the same as what he wore to work every day but without the pants legs.

Clare sighed. 'He's coming such a long way. We can wait for a few minutes.'

Jack wondered what Finn would be like. He'd met his cousin once, six years ago, when they were both eight. Jack and his mom had flown to Dublin when his aunt got married. He remembered the flight perfectly – the way the seat pushed against his back when they took off, the cotton puffs of cloud beneath them as they flew, the bumpy landing that scared him so much he had grabbed his mother's arm. He also remembered how rainy Dublin had been – even wetter than Seattle. But he couldn't remember anything about Finn.

Most of all Jack wondered about Finn's arm. What would *that* look like?

The international terminal at Sea-Tac Airport was bright and airy, with huge viewing windows and a full-scale replica of a P-51 Mustang fighter plane hanging from the ceiling. A P-51 was the first model Jack had ever assembled, an all-balsa-wood 1-32 scale with USAF decals that his dad gave him on his tenth birthday. He had painted it silver and blue and installed it on the top shelf of the glass display case in his bedroom. It was still his favourite, and the replica was the main reason he liked coming to the airport. Though he was curious about Finn, too.

His dad returned and stared at the screen, arms folded across his chest. He spoke to Jack's mom without looking at her. 'When was the last time you saw him?'

'When I was home for Oonagh's wedding.'

His mom had been living in Seattle for twenty years, but she still called Ireland 'home'.

'What was he like?'

She glanced at Jack. 'A nice boy. Intelligent. Happy.'

'Well, he ain't happy now.' He spoke under his breath but loud enough for Jack to hear. Usually, his parents didn't talk like this in front of him, but when his dad was annoyed he'd say anything. Anything except swear words.

'Will you recognise him?'

'I don't know.'

But when Finn walked through the arrivals gate, pale and blinking and looking like he'd just got out of bed, they knew him at once. He was listening to his iPod and wearing the same clothes as in the photograph his mother, Orla, had sent them: knit stocking cap, black jeans and two black T-shirts – short-sleeve on top, with a green Xbox 360 logo on the front, and long-sleeve underneath, so that his arms, Jack was disappointed to see, were covered. He carried a scuffed rucksack and a plastic duty-free bag.

Jack's mom hugged Finn as he removed the headphones. 'You're very welcome,' she said.

He winced. His face was thin, and he had a lot of acne. He looked like one of the skateboarders who spent all day doing kickflips on the long sidewalk in front of the public library.

'Hey Finn, I'm Howard.' Jack's dad thrust out his hand and Finn shook it lightly. 'You remember your cousin Jack?'

The boys nodded at each other, awkward and embarrassed. And, as Jack could have predicted, it was about to get worse. His dad, who worked for Microsoft, was staring at the Xbox logo on Finn's shirt.

'360, huh?' He stuck a meaty thumb in the air and grinned like a game-show host. 'Live your moment.'

Jack stared at the fighter plane.

***

3

'I didn't ask to come here.'

Finn said this to Jack as soon as they were alone in the bedroom. He sat on the upper bunk, his legs dangling over the side. His jeans had hiked up his legs, revealing shins as white as a fish's belly. The air conditioning was off and the house was warm, but he'd kept his hat on and his sleeves down.

'I didn't say you did.'

'It's not my fault my mum hasn't a clue.'

It was bad enough that Jack's mom had told him he had to share his bedroom with Finn, even though there were two empty guest rooms in the house, but she also made him give up his bed. He had slept in the top bunk since he was nine. The only reason he had bunk beds in the first place was for sleepovers, and he hadn't had one of those in two years.

'Where'd you get all those?' Finn asked, pointing at the display case full of models.

'I made them.'

'You *made* them?'

'Assembled them. Painted them. Put the decals on.'

'That meant to be your hobby?'

'I guess.'

Jack suddenly saw his room through Finn's eyes: not just the models but the Seahawks and Mariners pennants, the math and spelling trophies, the honour roll certificates that his mom had framed and hung on the wall, the posters detailing the zones of the solar system and the instruments of the orchestra. It was a nerd's room, accomplished and instructive, everything in its place.

'D'you have an Xbox?' Finn said.

'No.'

'PlayStation? Nintendo?'

'My parents think gaming is a waste of time.'

Finn snorted and nodded at the models. 'And those aren't?'

There were dark circles under his eyes. Beneath the corners of his jaw were clusters of acne that looked raw and sore.

'You have a computer at least?'

'I use the one in the kitchen,' Jack said.

'Your oul' fella not trust you?'

'My what?'

'Howard. Your dad.'

'I get a laptop when I start high school.'

'When's that?'

'In September.'

Finn lifted his legs onto the bed and flopped back so that his face was hidden. He was quiet for so long that Jack thought he'd fallen asleep. Then he said, 'What games you got on that desktop out there?'

'Like I said. My parents …'

Another silence. 'Right,' Finn said at last. 'First thing we do is get *that* sorted.'

After dinner, Jack's dad went to work in his study and his mom took the two boys to Cold Stone Creamery for dessert. On the way she asked a stream of questions about

Finn's mother, his two younger sisters, how he liked some place called Balbriggan, how the Dublin Gaelic football team was doing. He answered with as few words as possible, staring out the car window and plucking at the sleeves of his T-shirt and the seams of his jeans. Soon there was total silence. Finn took his iPod from his pocket and inserted the earbuds. As Jack's mom drove, her eyes flicked back and forth from the road to the rear-view mirror, angled so that she could see Finn in the back seat.

Halfway into his ice-cream, Finn said he wasn't feeling well, so they drove back to the house. It was jetlag, Jack's mom said. Finn's body clock was still on Irish time and it would be a few days before he adjusted. Remember when we went to Ireland, she said to Jack, how sick you got on the way from the airport? Her voice had that bright, false tone it got when she was worried. It was a tone that prompted a gnawing in Jack's stomach, as if her concerns were his as well.

But he couldn't have cared less about Finn's body clock. All he worried about was having this strange kid in the bed above him for the next two months. So what if it was his cousin? It wasn't fair.

At home Finn had a shower and went to bed. Jack's mom went to her room to make some phone calls and his dad popped out of the study to tell him he had to work late. He was super busy, he said. All that time at the airport when next week Microsoft was rolling out a new operating system. He spoke rapidly, hands on his hips, his face coiled in a tight grimace, as if he would rather not be working, as if Microsoft wasn't always rolling out something.

The Mariners were playing at home against the White Sox, and Jack watched the last half of the game on TV. His favourite player, Ichiro Suzuki, had a great game and the Mariners won, 4-3. After the game, he fed the cat, watered the deck flowers, and rolled up the garden hose. From beyond the line of cottonwoods at the end of the yard he could hear a motor boat on Lake Washington. The night was clear and warm, and he left the windows open for his dad to close later. He ate a bowl of cereal. He dragged out each task for as long as he could, but eventually he had to say good night to his parents and go into his bedroom.

The sound of Finn's breathing rose and fell across the blare of crickets through the open window. There was a strange, slightly sour smell in the room, and the clothes Finn had been wearing that day were draped over his footboard. Jack did not turn on the lamp, but stood beside the bunks, allowing his eyes to adjust to the murk. The nightlight beside his desk glowed green, and after a few moments he saw that Finn's bare left arm was outside the bedclothes.

He waited for a while, then slipped off his shoes and stepped onto the side rail of the lower bunk, so that his head was high enough to lean across and examine Finn's arm. Holding his breath, he looked closely. He could feel a thumping in his chest. On the underside of the forearm he could just make out a symbol that had been literally carved into the skin. The scabs of the wound, enflamed at the edges, formed a cross, topped by three pointed slashes like the imprint of a bird's foot.

As Jack stared at the symbol, Finn suddenly swivelled his head so that their faces were within inches of each other. He was wide awake.

'What are you at?' Finn said.

Jack jumped down from the rail. 'I'm just going to bed.'

Finn slid his arm under the bedsheet. His pale skin shone in the greenish light and his eyes were like dark stones.

'It's all a big show, isn't it?'

'What is?'

'Me. The Finn Geraghty show. The freak from Dublin.'

'I'm sorry. I just wanted to see what it looks like.'

'Well, you've had a good goo now, so you have, but you know what? You'll never get inside my head. You'll never know that story.'

'I don't want to know.'

'Everyone thinks they know my story. But they know fuck all.'

He turned in the bed, faced the wall and pulled the covers over his head.

2.

Jack did know the story – or the bones of it, anyway. He had heard his parents discussing it while he studied in his room. He'd also overheard his mother talking to his aunt on the phone and read the seven-page letter from Finn's mom that was left lying on the kitchen table. That was a funny thing about his parents – they made a big deal out of telling him there were certain things he was too young to know, then made it easy for him to find those things out.

Finn was a 'problem child'. At least that was the phrase his dad used. His mom disagreed.

'They don't use that term anymore,' she'd said. 'It's not politically correct.'

'What is he, then?'

'He's vulnerable.'

'We're *all* vulnerable.'

'It's a clinical label, Howard.'

Finn had developed a compulsion for video games. Or one in particular called *Gang Feud 3*. He was so obsessed that his mother was in despair. 'He has stopped doing anything except playing this game,' she wrote. 'He's not involved in any sport, has no hobbies and hasn't done a tap of schoolwork in over six months. His Junior Cert is next year and he has me driven mental. I don't know what to do and neither do his teachers.'

Finn had been a good student in primary school, but

he had failed every subject in his Easter exams. He was surly and uncommunicative. Often, he pretended to be sick, staying home from school and gaming all day while his mother was at work. The only boys he hung around with were other gamers who couldn't wait to get home to play online.

Gang Feud 3 was rated M for Mature, so even if Jack's parents had allowed him to play video games he would not have played this one. But he'd heard kids talking about it at school. After choosing a gang to belong to, each player went through an initiation ceremony, which included running for a drug dealer, stealing a car and hiring a prostitute. Once you were accepted into your gang, you got the appropriate tattoos and cruised the streets in a lowrider Chevy Impala, selling drugs and buying guns. You scored points by making sales and extending your gang's territory, which involved killing policemen and rival gang members. Triple points were awarded for targeted assassinations. You could use points to pimp your vehicle and enhance your weapons. Score enough and you moved up the gang hierarchy, from soldier to lieutenant to captain to warlord. Needless to say, the game was laden with foul language.

Finn's dad had not been on the scene for many years. He was certainly long gone by the time Jack and his mother had visited Ireland. By then, Jack's aunt, Orla, was back using her maiden name, and she'd also had the children's names legally changed to Geraghty. Jack couldn't remember their old name, if he knew it in the first place.

He did remember a phrase his mom had once used about her sister's ex-husband: 'a nasty piece of work'. When she said this, a look had crossed her face that Jack had never seen before.

Aunt Orla was a solicitor, which is what they called a lawyer in Ireland, and because the Irish economy wasn't doing so well, she had time on her hands. At least that's what she said in her letter. But she was more comfortable doing stuff with Finn's two younger sisters than with her son. Most evenings and weekends she was out, bringing the girls to piano or Irish dancing or drama. They were high achievers. That left Finn with plenty of time to perfect his gang skills and work towards being a warlord. 'It's not that I didn't give him every chance,' Orla wrote, 'or that I'm not hoarse from telling him to do what's best for himself. I've tried everything I can think of to make him see what he's missing. Over the last year he's lost all respect for me, and whenever I say anything to him the whole thing turns into a shouting match. Which is why I finally went to his year head.'

'What's a year head?' Jack's dad had asked his mom.

It was late at night. Jack was still awake and could hear them through the open bedroom door.

'Sort of an academic advisor,' his mom said.

'What'd he do?'

'According to Orla, he called Finn in to his office and laid it all out. Told him that these video games were damaging his schoolwork and social life, alienating him from his family, desensitising him to violence.'

'I'm not sure I buy that argument.'

'Well, Howard, *something's* the matter with him. Wait till I tell you. At the beginning of May, the school told him he had a month to get his act together. Otherwise they weren't going to let him do the Junior Cert. So what does he do?'

Jack's mom dropped her voice. He had to strain to hear her from behind his bedroom door.

'He carved a gang symbol into his forearm. With a penknife.'

'You're kidding me.'

'I am not. In history class. The boy sitting beside him fainted when he saw the blood, so the teacher thought something had happened to the boy who passed out. They called an ambulance, gave the boy first aid and so forth. Meanwhile, Finn was hiding the wound. Until the boy woke up and said what *really* happened.'

'Then what?'

'Well, according to the year head – not that Orla believes everything he says – the nurse who dressed Finn's wound told the principal about the thing on his arm and they called him down for an explanation. But he went mad in the principal's office and had to be restrained. Cursing at the top of his voice, ripping the dressing off the wound, punching the year head in the chest.'

'Sheesh.'

'By the time Orla got there he was screaming and waving his arms and blood was flying everywhere.'

Finn was suspended from school for the remainder of

the term and Orla arranged counselling for him at the Family First Centre. There was talk of boot camps, behaviour modification programmes, residential treatment facilities. 'All these things sound awful to me,' Orla had said in the letter. 'But the counsellors say he needs a change of scene and a disciplined environment where he has no access to these games and where positive male role models can give him direction. They tell me that summer is a high-risk period for vulnerable boys and I'm worried sick.'

Jack's mom came up with the idea of inviting Finn to Seattle. Jack's dad was against it at first, but she worked on him until he agreed. Though even then he didn't sound too happy about it.

'So he comes over,' his dad said, 'and I'm expected to give him direction. Like I don't have enough to do.'

'You're a *role* model. He observes you in your role as father and worker and it will be good for him. You don't have to *do* anything. Just be yourself.'

During this conversation, Jack couldn't see his dad, but he could picture his face: forehead crinkled, eyes flicking back and forth, mouth small and hard. Like he looked when they visited his aunt's family and his uncle Jeff, who owned a lumber mill, wondered out loud what exactly it was that Jack's dad did for a living.

'You're saying he's vulnerable. What makes you think he won't be vulnerable here? You trying to tell me he can't get into trouble in Seattle?'

'It's a settled family environment. With supervision and

none of the temptation he has at home. No video games and plenty of other things to do – there's the parks pro-gramme and softball and he can do the sailing camp if he wants. He'll also have Jack.'

She dropped her voice. Jack moved to his bedroom door, which was open an inch or two, and listened closely. 'Seeing a well-adjusted boy in the family might help him. And you know it might help Jack as well.'

'What help does he need?'

'Maybe being with someone his own age for a change will help him understand a few things.'

'Understand what? The kid's sharp as a tack.'

'He's good at schoolwork.'

'He's good at everything. He never needs my help. Never asks for it.'

'You're always working.'

'How else is all this going to get paid for?'

'It's just that he's too … protected,' his mom said. 'And maybe a little … well, he does get everything he wants.'

'No he doesn't. He has a job. He works for his pocket money. If anyone spoils him, *you* do.'

Now it was his mom's face that Jack could picture: the way her eyes narrowed and her chin lifted when she tried to convince him that something she really wanted was what *he* wanted.

'Maybe I do,' she said. 'I just think it will be good for him to have to share a little. And anyway, it's only for a couple of months.'

There was a long silence.

'I don't know,' his dad had said. 'You really think we can help this boy?'

'Look, anything's better than where he is now. And think about Orla. If something doesn't change she's going to end up in John of God's.'

'What's that?'

'A loony bin.'

'Whoa. Whatever happened to politically correct?'

3.

Jack earned pocket money from his paper route, which he had inherited six months ago from his next-door neighbour, Jimmy Choi. He delivered the *Post-Intelligencer* to forty-three houses in West Bellevue, from SE 8th Street to Killarney Glen Park. It was a lot of ground to cover, even on his new bike, but routes were more and more spread out these days. His dad said it was because of the internet. Newspapers are on the way out, he said. Who's going to pay for something they can get online for nothing? Then why, Jack wanted to ask him back, did you make me take the job?

The route took over an hour, and as weekday papers had to be delivered by six a.m., Jack was up at half past four – half past five on Sunday. Winter had been tough, but now that summer was here the early rise wasn't so bad: the mornings warm, the birds twittering, the sun rising like a huge basketball over the hills beyond Redmond. And with school out, he could go back to bed when he was finished and sleep for a few more hours.

The worst thing about the job was collecting from his customers, which he had to do once a month. Even if he collected on a Tuesday evening – his dad told him that Tuesday was the night of the week when most people stayed home – he was lucky to get twenty-five payments. So he had to do the circuit several times in the days that followed, hoping he'd finish before he got his own bill from the paper. Some people took four or five visits, and there were always a few who were *never* in, which meant they carried the debt into the following month and cut into his profits. If everybody paid on time, Jack made $140 a month, which would've been pretty good if all he had to do was deliver.

Then his mom got the bright idea for Finn to help with the route and scoop half the money. They'd had an argument about it two days before Finn's arrival.

'It's not fair.'

'Of course it's fair – he does half the work, you give him half the money.'

'But I don't want to give him *any* work. It's my route.'

He was clearing the table while she filled the dishwasher. His dad was working late.

'You're always complaining that it takes too long,' she said. 'This way you'll finish twice as fast.'

'Once I'm up that early, it really doesn't matter how long it takes. My morning's already ruined.'

'I didn't know it was such a burden for you.'

'I only took the route because Dad made me.'

'You seem pretty happy with the money. You'll be able to buy that telescope.'

Sometimes he thought she made stupid statements just to get him mad.

'If I have to give what's-his-name half,' he said, 'then I *won't* be able to get the telescope.'

'Finn. His name is Finn. He's your first cousin.'

'What about collecting?'

She paused, a dirty plate in her hand. 'Family is important. It's not like we wanted an only child but that's how it worked out, and that's fine, of course, but now you have an opportunity to see what it's like to share with, you know, someone who's like a brother.'

She was almost breathless after this rush of words. He didn't like what she said. Especially the word 'brother'.

'What about collecting?' he repeated.

'What about it?'

'Will he help me with that?'

'No sense the pair of you doing it. Sure, it's only one night a month.'

'*Mom*. It could be a whole week. It's the hardest part of the job.'

'Jack, the decision's made and you're going to share the route. And the money. And your room and your bike and your weights and everything else you're so lucky and blessed to have. That's *final*.'

She slammed shut the dishwasher door and left the kitchen.

But he didn't have to share his bike because the next day his dad brought one home for Finn. 'Only second-hand,' he said, to make Jack feel better; the courier on the Microsoft campus had upgraded and didn't need it anymore. But it was as good as Jack's new bike, which really wasn't that new anyway – he'd got it last Christmas after begging for one for three years.

Finn joined Jack on the route the morning after he

arrived; he was awake at four anyway because of the time difference. Not that he did anything. He cycled alongside, out of breath, while Jack explained how to fold the paper in on itself and how each customer wanted his delivery a certain way: on the porch, behind the screen door, in the mailbox or newspaper box with the gothic *Post-Intelligencer* script stencilled along the side. But Finn didn't listen very carefully, and on Sunday morning he didn't even get out of bed.

His mom couldn't do enough for the boys that first week. She took them sailing on Lake Union and rock climbing in Ballard. They visited the aquarium and toured the baseball stadium, went to the top of the Space Needle and had lunch at Pike Place Market. His dad was getting ready for a week-long business trip to New York, but the Sunday before he left he took them to a Mariners game. He also promised to bring Finn to the division in Microsoft where they designed the Xbox, but he wasn't able to arrange it before he left.

Finn didn't show much appreciation for all this activity. He told Jack that the rock climbing was pointless and the Space Needle even more boring than the spire on O'Connell Street, whatever that was. The only time all week he got excited was when they came out of the aquarium and a group of Latino kids swaggered past on Alaskan Way, wearing baggy T-shirts and jeans, trucker hats and chunky silver jewellery. A couple of them had tattoos on their forearms. Finn's face lit up as they swayed past, speaking Spanish and swinging their arms ghetto-style.

'That's *so* cool,' he said. Whether he was aware of it or not, he was rubbing the scar on his own forearm.

His mom glanced from the Latinos to Finn. 'You're not in Dublin now.'

'I know.'

'There's no messing with those lads.'

But Finn was raptly following their progress up the street, the roll of their shoulders and the shuffle of their untied sneakers.

On Sunday, after the game, his dad grilled steaks and they ate on the deck. Light from the setting sun filtered through the cottonwood trees and the crickets were in full chorus. His mom had lit a citronella candle to keep away mosquitoes. His dad was on his second beer with dinner, and he'd had one at the game. As usual on the night before he travelled, he was in a good mood.

'So, boys,' he said. 'How's the route going? Sunday's a heavy day.'

'Not so bad,' Finn said, before Jack could answer.

'Many hands make light work,' his mom said.

'Division of labour.' His dad blinked and stared at Finn. 'You enjoy the game?'

'I liked the hot dogs.'

'You'll learn. Baseball is America's pastime. I love that kid Betancourt. The Cuban. Real speed.'

'I like Suzuki,' Jack said.

'I know you do.'

'It's meant to be the all-American game,' his mom said to Finn, allowing her Irish accent to thicken, 'but all the players speak Spanish. Or Japanese.'

'Not Sexson,' his dad said. 'He's from right here in Washington. Six foot eight. They don't make 'em that big in Japan.'

Something about the conversation wasn't right, as if Jack's parents were saying things just to keep Finn in the flow. Or to fill the space left by his silence. His mom had given each of the boys a can of Coke, which usually wasn't allowed at dinner.

'About the route,' Finn said, looking at the plate. 'It's not really going any quicker.'

This remark took Jack by surprise.

'Why not?' his dad said.

'The two of us just ride along, like, and do the same thing. It'd be loads faster if we split it, and each did half.'

Jack's dad looked at him.

'I'm showing him what to do,' Jack said.

'I *know* what to do. It doesn't take a week to learn how to fold a newspaper.'

His dad wiped his mouth with a paper napkin. 'He's got a point, Jack.'

Jack wanted to say that Finn *couldn't* fold a newspaper; that he wanted to toss papers on the move, from the bike onto the porch like they did in the movies, even though it wasn't allowed; that he had skipped delivery that morning, the one day in the week when he knew his dad wouldn't be up early for work. This kid was sneaky, and Jack didn't trust him. But if he said any of this he would be told to go to his room.

'This is a partnership,' his mom said.

Jack didn't say anything.

'It'll be win-win,' his dad said. 'You get the route done quicker and Finn makes a few bucks. American style.'

In a small voice, Jack said, 'Any complaints come in, they'll be my responsibility.'

'And that's why,' his dad said, winking at Finn, 'your Irish cousin is going to do a fantastic job. Right, Finn?'

'Right,' Finn said, glancing Jack's way with the slightest of smirks.

'What were you lying for?'

'About what?'

'The route.'

'I didn't lie.'

'You told my dad you helped me this morning.'

'I didn't say that.'

'Sunday is the one day I could use the help. The papers are, like, ten times heavier.'

'You won't let me help. I just ride along like a spare tool.'

'You could've carried the papers at least.'

'So don't pay me for Sunday.'

The boys lay in bed, lights out. The underside of the top bunk had a green tinge from the nightlight, and the mattress bulged slightly between the slats from the pressure of Finn's body. That bulge infuriated Jack.

'You don't have to do it, you know.'

'I want to,' Finn said.

'You want the money.'

'Your mum asked me to help out; I'm helping out.'

'My *mom*, I call her *mom*.'

'Such a fucking moaner.'

Jack leaned out from the lower bunk. '*What* did you say?'

'You heard me.'

'I'm telling my mom.'

'Telling her what?'

'That you swore.'

Finn laughed slowly, and the bulge in the mattress dipped further. 'Go on then, tell her. Tell your *mum*. Like I give a shite.'

4.

Jack's dad was an early riser: in the kitchen by six, making coffee and mixing his own granola with fruit he dried in a food dehydrator in the basement. The week before his New York trip, he worked from home, so he was around the house, trotting from his study to the kitchen to his bedroom, frowning and protesting with a raised hand that he could not be interrupted, that he had a million things to do before flying out on Monday morning. When he left, the house immediately adopted a quieter rhythm, especially in the early morning, when Jack and Finn returned from delivering papers. Jack's mom didn't get up until eight, sometimes nine.

On Tuesday morning, as they hung their newspaper pouches on the coat hooks beside the door to the deck, Finn said to Jack, 'Let's go online.'

Jack was not allowed to use the family computer without supervision. Even when his mom did let him use it, he could only access the internet to do schoolwork or research something educational. This definition could be stretched at times to include baseball highlights or a YouTube music video, but only with special permission.

'We're not allowed.'

'But your mum's fast asleep.'

'She might hear.'

'We'll keep the volume down.'

'No. I'll get in big trouble.'

24

But Finn was already logging on, and the beeps and whirrs of the hard drive sounded as loud to Jack as dogs baying in the back yard. Jack closed the kitchen door. Figuring it was safer to monitor Finn than leave him to it, he pulled up a chair.

'Jays', Windows 7,' Finn said, the mouse scurrying over the pad and panes of information popping up all over the desktop. 'Your oul' fella must get all the latest apps for free, right?'

'I guess.'

'Eighty gigs of space and you haven't even used ten. What a waste.'

'OK, you've had a look, let's shut it down and go back to bed.'

But to Jack's dismay, Finn was trawling through a Google search for *Gang Feud 3*, opening windows faster than Jack could read their banners. Finn's awkwardness riding a bike or throwing a baseball had been replaced at the keyboard by smoothness and assurance. Another flurry of clicks, more flapping from the hard drive and he leaned back in his chair and smiled. 'How 'bout some cereal?'

'Are you finished?'

'In a minute.'

Nervous, Jack poured two bowls of Cheerios. Something was happening on the screen. Percentages whizzing from 0 to 100, dialogue boxes opening and closing, permissions sought and granted. This was not good.

'Listen,' Jack said, 'we're going to eat the cereal and then turn it off.'

'Do you have a credit card?' Finn asked.

'You're kidding, right?'

'Does your mum have one we could borrow? I can pay her back when you pay me for the route.'

'Why do you want a credit card?'

Finn tapped the monitor with a knuckle. 'For this.'

'Are you crazy?'

Tucking into the cereal, Finn launched a demo he had downloaded of *Gang Feud 3*. Onscreen, its introductory film clip showed three gang members breaking down the door of a house in a ghetto neighbourhood. The images were animated but very realistic, and the characters dressed and walked like the boys Finn had admired outside the aquarium. Once in the house, they drew guns and moved through a series of empty rooms, speaking in short, heavily accented sentences that Jack found hard to follow.

'This *vato* likely armed, man, all AK'd.'

'Let's bang.'

'Don't bone out on me.'

His mouth full of Cheerios, Finn laughed – a rich, sat-isfied laugh that was new to Jack. A stream of milk ran down his chin and dripped onto his T-shirt.

'Turn it *down*,' Jack said. But he watched the screen closely.

The gang members came to a closed door. Rap music blared behind it. The three men gathered round the door, lifted their guns and cocked them with sliding, metallic clicks. The leader made a hand sign to the others and they smashed into the room. The music grew louder. Opposite the door, a man in a string vest and camouflage pants sat on a floor-level mattress smoking a plastic pipe, while on either side of him two women with hardly any clothes on stroked his shoulders. As soon as he saw the gangsters, the man pushed the women aside and grabbed a machine gun propped against the wall. But, too quick for him, the gang boys opened fire, and his body twitched and jumped and pumped blood all over the mattress while the women screamed and the guns roared and Finn cackled with glee.

The sound was thunderous. Jack fiddled with the speaker knobs, trying to turn down the volume as the dust settled onscreen.

'Watch this,' Finn said.

The gang leader pushed the body aside and picked up a big bag of white powder from the floor. The women cowered, but the man sneered at them, spat on the body and said to the others, '*Vamos.*'

'*Vamos,*' Finn repeated, grinning and staring at the screen. His face was flushed with excitement, and the patch of acne below his jawline pulsed in the rinsed morning light. 'Omar, my man, you are so down for the hood.'

The door opened and Jack's mom leaned in, holding her bathrobe closed by the lapels. Her hair was mussed and her eyes puffy. 'Boys? What are you doing?'

Jack popped out of the chair. 'Oh, hi Mom.'

'What's that racket?'

'What racket?'

'Are you on the computer? What time is it?'

'I don't know. We're just having some cereal.'

She came into the kitchen, frowning and tightening the

belt of her robe. 'Jack, what have I said about – '

'Aunt Clare,' Finn said, 'have a look at this.'

Oh no, Jack thought, what is he doing now?

She peered at the computer. All trace of the game had vanished; instead, the screen held a picture of a long, Oriental-looking boat manned by a dozen oarsmen.

'What's that?' she said.

'They're called dragon boats. They have them on Lake Union.'

'Yes, I've heard about those.'

'You can get lessons. Jack told me about them so I thought we'd check online. Can him and me get lessons?'

'He and I.'

'The sailing was cool, like, but this looks brilliant.'

She shrugged, rubbed her eyes. 'Today?'

'Maybe next week. When Uncle Howard gets back.'

'I was thinking maybe the art camp next week, but if you'd prefer this …'

'You want some cereal, Mom?'

She smoothed her hair and blinked in the bright light from the window. 'No. I'm going to have a shower.'

Finn switched off the PC and brought his cereal bowl to the sink. She headed back to her room but stopped at the door. 'Jack?'

'Yes, Mom?'

'Next time ask permission. To use the computer.'

'Oh. Yeah. Sure.'

***

Jack gave Finn the southern half of the paper route, below 16th. It had slightly fewer customers, but it was the tougher half, with hills and dead ends and houses widely spaced out. They divided up the papers at Jack's house and cycled down Bellevue Way as far as the Minimart, where they went their separate ways. When they completed delivery they met beside the tennis courts at Killarney Glen Park.

From the beginning Finn was finished first. Every time. Jack couldn't understand it. He was a faster cyclist, knew the route better and had the easy half. But no matter how hard Jack pushed himself, Finn was at the courts first, leaning casually against the chain-link fence as if he had been there for hours.

'You're not putting the papers where they should go,' Jack said.

'I am so.'

'You couldn't be. How do you get done so fast?'

'Why are you so slow? That's what I want to know.'

'I'm *not* slow. I just make sure I do a good job.'

'So do I.'

The park held a summer tennis camp, and the two instructors arrived at six. Sometimes the boys stayed and watched them warm up. The two men were semi-pros from the Seattle Athletic Club, and they could really smoke the ball. One of them knew Jack's dad, who was a member of the club.

Jimmy Choi was at the camp, as well as Brandon Eberhardt and Zach Lopach, who had attended Jack's school but were a year ahead. They started at seven, and on Friday Jack and Finn were still at the courts when they arrived.

'Hey, paperboy,' Jimmy said. 'Still losing money on my route?'

'It's not your route, it's mine. And I'm making money.'

'Only half of what you should, is what I hear.'

Jimmy glanced at Finn, who was hanging back, wary, his fingers looped through the diamonds of the fence mesh. From the court, regular as a metronome, came the solid *pock-pock* of the ball being hit by the instructors. The sun, which had burned off the early-morning haze, warmed the park's fir trees, stirring their scent.

'My cousin is helping me. Just for two months.'

Zach and Brandon stared at Finn. Country-club kids, they wore designer tennis whites and carried their three-hundred-dollar rackets in brightly coloured tourney bags. They were heavy set and deeply tanned, though it was only June. Finn was all in black: knit cap, frayed T-shirt, track-suit pants, Converse basketball shoes. He looked gaunt and unhealthy, with a fresh rash of pimples blooming on his forehead.

'Are you from Ireland?' Zach said.

'Yeah.'

'You speak English?'

Brandon guffawed. Jimmy slapped Zach with his baseball cap. 'You moron.'

Zach grabbed the cap and threw it over the fence. Jimmy watched it fall to the court surface and said to Finn,

'Everything these guys know about Ireland, they know from a cereal box.'

'They're always after me Lucky Charms,' Zach said in the stage-Irish voice of a television ad.

'You don't look Irish,' Brandon said.

'What's an Irish lad meant to look like?' Finn answered.

His reedy voice and defensive tone seemed to surprise the boys, and they didn't answer.

'You guys should join the camp,' Jimmy said, nodding at the instructors, who had finished their warm-up and were towelling down. 'Alex is a great teacher.'

He said this loud enough for Alex to hear.

'I don't have a racket,' Finn said.

'Brandon will give you one. He's got about a million. Right, Brandon?'

Brandon popped his gum and pointed at Jimmy's hat, lying on the court like a dead bird.

As they cycled home, Finn said to Jack, '*They* had a good laugh.'

'I didn't hear anyone laughing.'

'That Chinese lad is the only who one has a clue.'

'Jimmy's not Chinese. He's Korean-American.'

'What does that make you – Irish-American?'

'Half. My dad is Norwegian and Slovenian.'

Finn raised himself off the saddle and spat onto the road. 'You're all Yanks to me,' he said and, with a burst of speed, pulled ahead, pedalling furiously.

The next morning, Finn was not at the tennis courts when Jack finished the route, and he felt a pulse of satisfaction at being first. It was before six, and the courts were empty. He leaned his bike against the fencing and listened to the birds, savouring the solitude. High in the pale sky was a criss-cross of vapour trails. The air was very clear, with a strange sort of shimmer, as if the passing jets had let loose a fall of microscopic glitter.

After a few minutes he heard a low whistle and saw Finn standing in a grove of firs to the left of the club-house. He got his bike and went over to him. Finn's bike was in a heap on the ground. He held an open quart of chocolate milk in his hand.

'What are you doing over here?' Jack said.

'Watching you. Waiting for your tennis friends?'

'I was waiting for you.'

'Thought you'd finished first, didn't you?'

'It's not a competition.'

'It isn't?'

Finn took a swig of the milk, which left a streak of brown above his upper lip.

'Where'd you get the milk?' Jack asked.

'From the shops.'

'The Minimart doesn't open until seven.'

'Not that shop. A different one.'

'Where?'

Finn shrugged and held out the carton. 'Want some?'

Jack looked at the dirt under his fingernails, the thin greasy hair poking out from beneath the knit cap, the scar on his forearm. 'No.'

Finn poured what remained onto the dense bed of

pine needles at his feet. It splashed onto Jack's shoes.

'What are you *doing*?' Jack shouted, leaping back.

'You said you didn't want any.'

'That's littering. And a waste.'

'A *waste*?'

Finn kicked the milk-soaked needles and a clump stuck to Jack's pants. He shook it off and got back on his bike. 'Don't think you're going online when we get back.'

'Who's going to stop me?'

'I'll wake my mom. I'll tell her you're downloading adult stuff.'

His accent remarkably accurate, Finn imitated the demo voiceover: '*This playable demo of* Gang Feud 3 *is rated E for Everyone.*'

'Shut up. I'm leaving.'

'Going to play tennis?'

'No, I'm going home.'

He cycled off, willing Finn not to follow.

'That's right,' Finn yelled. 'Run home to *mommy*.'

5.

With Finn in the house, the meals grew more adventurous: quesadillas with homemade salsa, southern fried chicken, tuna steaks marinated in lime, smoked fish chowder. And Jack's mom was baking again – pumpkin bread and apple tart and chocolate chip cookies – something she hadn't done since Jack was in the fourth grade, when she was on the parent-teacher association and ran the school bake sales.

Finn liked the desserts, all right, but Jack noticed that he rarely finished his dinner; somehow the family rule imposed on Jack all his life had been relaxed. Of course, Finn acted as if he just *loved* everything that Clare made, and for the week that Jack's dad was gone he kept oiling her down with praise for her cooking and comments about how he never got meals like that at home.

'Have you noticed,' she said to Jack one evening while Finn was in the shower, 'how his manners have improved? See what a change of scene and a little bit of positive attention can do for a young man?'

Jack didn't answer, not just because he knew the truth, but also because it was one of those questions his mom didn't want him to answer. It was her way of teaching him a lesson while pretending she was asking for his opinion. She did it all the time.

Jack figured Finn was up to something, and the reason

for the compliments emerged on Thursday, after dinner. When they had finished filling the dishwasher and sweeping the floor, Clare asked Jack to get a bag of compost from the trunk of her car and put it in the back yard so she could do some potting. When he returned to the kitchen, he saw her leaning over the table, peering at a copy of one of the tabloid newspapers you got free at the Minimart. Finn had opened the paper and was showing her a colourful display ad. Jack could tell from the hunch in her shoulders that she did not like what she saw.

'It's like a big exhibition,' Finn said. 'They have all these cool cars there, and you just walk around and, like, look at them and stuff.'

She didn't say anything. Jack edged in. The full-page ad showed a range of modified cars and trucks with jacked-up suspensions, wide fender skirts, chrome wheels and whitewall tyres. Women in bikinis with big lips and sultry expressions sat on the hoods or leaned against the doors. The vehicles had been custom-painted in garish colours and decorated with pinstripes and airbrushed murals and stylised licks of flame. Along the bottom of thepage, in big yellow letters, was INTERNATIONAL LOWRIDER AUTO SHOW. There were also some sentences in Spanish. The show was on that coming weekend at the event centre at Qwest Field.

'I could get the bus in,' Finn said.

'I don't think so,' Clare murmured.

'Or maybe you could drop me off?'

Finn made eye contact with Jack, his look poised between pleading and contempt. All week, in spite of Jack's protests and threats, he had been using the computer when his mom was asleep or out of the house. He surfed the internet, downloaded demos and accessed file-sharing sites to get new songs for his iPod. Sometimes, when Jack complained, Finn called him a sap; other times he tried to get on his good side. Either way, Jack didn't care, but so far he had held back from saying anything to his mom. She would probably end up blaming him anyway.

'I don't think so,' she repeated, frowning as she lifted her head from the page. Jack could tell she didn't like refusing Finn, but neither did she like the look of those women in the skimpy swimsuits.

'Please, Aunt Clare, *please*. Just for an hour. It's such a cool show.'

'It's downtown; it's on the weekend. The type of people you get at these things ...'

'What type of people? It's an auto show. It's for people who like *cars*. It's like going to the aquarium.'

'We're invited to the Chois on Sunday. For a barbecue.'

'This is on Saturday.'

'I'll think about it.'

He badgered her all evening and all the next day. If it had been Jack she would have lost her temper. Instead, she explained several times, in a reasonable voice, how she couldn't let a fourteen-year-old go into the city by himself. Howard was not back until Sunday morning and she had volunteered all her time that Saturday to help at a clean-water fundraiser at Union Bay.

But as Jack knew she would, she relented. With conditions, to make it sound as if she wasn't giving in. She told

Finn that he could go to the show if he took a taxi there and back and was home by five. And Jack, she said, would have to go as well.

'But I don't want to go.'

'It will be fun,' she said. 'Something you boys can do together.'

Finn stared at Jack, lizard-eyed and triumphant, his face lit up with his dumb smirk, which faded instantly to little-boy innocence whenever Jack's mom glanced his way.

'We do everything together,' Jack said.

'Finn's been helping you with the route and keeping you company, so it's no harm doing something *he'd* like for a change.'

Like illegal downloading, Jack thought. Or splashing chocolate milk all over my shoes. 'All we ever do is what he likes.'

'That's not true.'

'I was going to buy a model on Saturday.'

'It will be fun,' she said with finality. 'Like going to the aquarium.'

This ridiculous repetition of Finn's own phrase, a phrase she herself had raised her eyes at when Finn used it the day before, infuriated Jack. He ran to his room, shouting and slamming the door behind him, knowing that she would be down in a few minutes to chastise him, knowing that his dad would get an update over the phone that night (and that there would be a 'man-to-man' talk next week) and knowing he now had no choice but to go with his cousin to that stupid show, full of kids like Finn who listened to gangsta rap and covered themselves in tattoos and lived in miserable neighbourhoods and thought drug dealers were cool.

His summer was being ruined.

That evening, after his mom had taken Finn for ice-cream and left Jack at home as punishment for his tantrum ('It's so unlike you … I really want you to think about your behaviour'), Jack got a phone call from Mr. Frankovich, his route supervisor at the newspaper.

'Hey, sport.'

'Hello Mr. Frankovich.'

'Call me Don. You're making me feel like I'm a hundred years old.'

It would do no good to explain that Jack's dad didn't allow him to call adults by their first name.

'How're your sleuthing skills?' Mr. Frankovich said.

'My what?'

'Elementary, my dear Watson. Murder on the Orient Express. Colonel Mustard in the conservatory with the lead pipe.'

Jack waited. He was used to Mr. Frankovich talking gibberish before getting to the point.

'Need you to keep your eyes peeled,' he continued. 'Customers on your route have been complaining. Case of the missing milk cartons. Seen anything unusual?'

'Missing milk?'

'Stolen. Milkman's dropping it off, that's been established, but it's gone by the time these folks get up. Or at least the tastier flavours.'

As if he were the culprit, Jack's stomach tumbled with guilt. 'How did you find out?'

'Find out what?'

'That milk was stolen.'

'Mentioned to me in relation to another matter, also of concern. Hey, Jackie, you're my top guy in Bellevue, but you must have somebody pinch-hitting for you, am I right? You been on vacation or something?'

'My cousin's been helping me. He's from Ireland.'

This simple statement of fact felt like a betrayal.

'This cousin – it possible his aim could be off? Like maybe the paper ends up in a hedge? Or a mud puddle?'

'I guess it's possible.'

'Something you can take care of?'

'Yeah. I'll take care of it.'

'Hey, buddy. Like I said, you're my top guy.' There was a long pause. Mr. Frankovich cleared his throat. 'And you hear anything about that milk situation, you'll let me know, right?'

'Right, Mr. Frankovich.'

'Call me Don.'

He waited until they were both in the bedroom before saying anything. The night was warm and humid. Finn, who didn't like to shower too often, smelled of sweat and ice-cream. He sat in his underwear and a T-shirt in the upper bunk, leafing through a copy of *Lowrider* magazine. A moth knocked itself against the bulb of his wall lamp, casting fluttering shadows on the ceiling. On the cover of the magazine was a photograph of a woman in a miniskirt and a belly top standing in front of a Chevy Impala. She had her hip thrust out and a flower in her hair.

'My mom buy you that?' Jack said.

Finn didn't look up from the magazine. 'What do *you* think?'

Jack, who had no reading light in the lower bunk, sat at the desk, pretending to sort through his model catalogues. 'How was the ice-cream?'

'Brilliant.'

'Better than the chocolate milk?'

Finn turned the page, his eyes flicking in Jack's direction. In his American television voice he said, '*Nothing beats a cool quart of choco-milk from Vitamilk Dairies. Nutritious and delicious.*'

'Yeah. That's what the cops figure.'

'That it's nutritious and delicious?'

'That you stole it.'

'I didn't steal anything.'

'They *know*, Finn.'

'Who knows?'

'The people you took it from.'

'Why, because you told them?'

'No, because it's so easy to figure out. The milkman delivers at four, the paperboy comes at five, the people get up at six and their chocolate milk's missing. Oh, yeah, and their paper's stuck in a hedge.'

Finn laughed. 'Not at *that* house it wasn't.'

Jack got up from the desk, grabbed the magazine from

Finn's hands and flung it across the room.

'Cheers,' Finn said.

'I'm getting blamed, you know.'

'Good.'

Jack grabbed him by the sleeve of his T-shirt and dragged him to the edge of the bed. Finn slapped him on the side of the head. Rage rose in Jack's throat with a taste of salt and metal and his vision became fuzzy and narrow. He pulled so hard at the shirt that the sleeve ripped off and he fell back and knocked his knee against the desk. Jack got up and rushed towards the bed. Finn, who was on his back, kicked him full in the chest. Jack stumbled, lost his footing and crashed into the display case, his hand punching through its glass front with a sound like a car crash.

After this burst of noise and commotion, there was a strange moment of silence as Jack lay dazed on the floor. His knee hurt. Finn jumped down from the bunk.

'Jaysus,' he said, 'your hand.'

Jack looked at his right hand, which still clutched the torn sleeve.

'No,' Finn said. 'The other one.'

At the side of Jack's left wrist was a deep, ragged gash. Thick, blackish blood oozed out. There was no pain, but a cold, dead absence of feeling. Finn took off his torn T-shirt and, bending over, wrapped it around the wound. 'C'mon,' he said. 'Sit up. Careful. We better show this to your … your mom.'

***

When they returned from the hospital it was nearly one in the morning, and Jack's mom sent them straight to bed. Jack was shaky and exhausted. As he lay on his mattress, above the covers because of the heat, he watched the underside of the top bunk catch glints of green from the nightlight as Finn shifted above him. His bandaged wrist, which hadn't hurt at all since the fall, even when he was getting the stitches, now began to throb, in spite of the painkillers the doctor had given him.

The movement above him increased, followed by a regular thumping sound that shook both bunks.

'What are you doing?' Jack said.

When Finn didn't answer, Jack got out of bed, making sure not to bump his wound. Finn lay with his arms at his sides, rhythmically banging the back of his head against the wooden headboard.

'Don't do that. You'll hurt yourself.'

When he wouldn't stop, Jack stood on the bedrail, leaned over and put his good hand at the back of Finn's neck.

'Are you crazy?' Jack said.

'Yes. No, I'm sick. That's what I am. A sad, sick gobshite.'

'Don't say that about yourself.'

'That's what everyone else says.'

'No, they don't.'

'Like *you* know.'

Finn was close to tears. The room had cooled some, but the window was still open. Crickets chirped loudly and the drone of a passing aeroplane stitched the darkness. Jack kept his hand behind Finn's neck until he was sure he wasn't going to bang his head again. They were silent for a while.

'Is that why you carved that symbol on your arm?'

'I don't want to talk about that.'

'OK.'

Finn had put on his Xbox T-shirt to replace the one that was torn and bloodied. Its green letters glowed mutely in the darkness. He snuffled a few times.

'Why didn't you tell her?' Finn said at last.

'I'm not a tattletale.'

When the drama was over and the injury cared for, his mom had nodded as Jack told her that he and Finn had been wrestling when he slipped. *The boys are wrestling,* she would be thinking. *It's so good they're getting on.*

On the way home from the hospital, Finn had offered to do the whole paper route in the morning.

Jack got back into bed. He was drowsy. There was no more movement above, and just as Jack was dropping off to sleep, Finn said, 'I'm sorry.'

'All right.'

'And you won't have to worry about the papers anymore. Or the milk.'

'Whatever.'

6.

The boys went to the lowrider show on Saturday afternoon. The weather was sultry and thundery. His mom was able to drop them at the event centre after all. As they got out of the car, she told them to walk straight in, stay inside no later than five o'clock and go directly to the taxi rank when they were finished. She gave Jack fifty dollars to pay for their entry fee and the cab home.

Finn had dressed up: he wore an oversized pair of jeans that Jack had never seen before, heavy denim with copper rivets and a thick link chain that hung between two of the belt loops. At home he had kept the jeans hitched above his waist, but as soon as they were dropped off he let them fall over his skinny hips so that the waistband of his Calvin Klein underpants showed, as well as an inch or two of scarlet fabric. He also wore a bright red T-shirt with a silk-screened image of a grinning skull and a Dodgers cap with the flattened bill angled to the side.

Standing on the crowded sidewalk, gazing up at the centre marquee, Finn lifted his arms like a rapper and sneered. '*Bajito y suavecito*,' he said, grinning at Jack. 'Low and slow, dude.'

'Sure. Let's go inside.'

Saturday afternoon was the peak time for the event, and the admission line was long and slow. All attendees had to pass through a metal detector, and though the queue held a sprinkling of pale-faced older men and suburban high-school kids, most of those lined up were urban Hispanic kids and motorheads. There was a lot of jewellery and studwork and piercings on display, so the screening alarm kept sounding and many in the line had to swagger through the security arch several times. The more often a kid set off the alarm, it seemed, the cooler he was, and Jack half-expected someone to pull a gun from his boot as in the *Gang Feud 3* demo that Finn played every day. This air of potential danger added to the lobby's big-event buzz, a summer-in-the-city vibe that Jack had to admit was exciting.

Inside, the hall was air-conditioned to an almost uncomfortable chill, and the vast empty space beneath the domed ceiling made everything seem smaller and quieter than it should have been. The floor was neatly parcelled into vendor booths and corralled exhibition spaces occupied by the customised cars and trucks, their suspensions jacked high, their coats waxed and buffed to a high shine, their doors open on glossy interiors that smelled of air freshener and expensive leather. Set on tilted stands, the vehicles looked odd, displayed like works of art but surrounded by a tattooed crowd that jived and jostled along the wide aisles, marshalled by a corps of burly security men in navy blazers and micro-headsets. The hubbub of voices was interrupted every few minutes by throaty engine roars from the 'pit stop' in the middle of the hall, a competition space surrounded by terraced seating and bright signs advertising auto parts and accessories.

The boys bought Cokes and waded through the crowd. Jack had gone through a car-model phase in the fifth grade, assembling mostly late-sixties muscle cars using Revell kits, so he enjoyed the show more than he'd expected, especially when they came across a 1971 Dodge Challenger with a split grille and a HEMI V8 engine, painted the same shade of metallic blue as the model he'd built three years ago. But Finn wasn't looking at the cars much. Since arriving at the centre, his gait had evolved from an excited saunter to a bouncy strut to a full-on pimp roll, shoulders swaying, knees dipping, fingers splayed as he grooved to some rap tune playing in his head.

'How come you're walking that way?' Jack said.

'Gotta have attitude, man. Gotta look like you got some serious game going down.'

'Is that how they talk in Dublin?'

Whenever they passed a group of Hispanic kids – most of them dressed as Finn was – he watched them closely, either for further clues on movement or style or to gauge the effect the cut of his own figure might be having on them. But nobody was looking at him except Jack, who began to feel as if he was in a badly acted movie.

'Aren't you interested in the cars? I thought that's why we came here.'

'I am. They fly-ass.'

'Right.'

At four o'clock, they took seats in the pit stop to watch the finals of the 'hydraulic showdown', a competition where lowrider-owners used remote-control handsets to jolt the suspensions so their cars hopped up and down and back and forth while the wide wheels bounced and the engines revved. The cheers of the crowd competed with hip-hop blaring from giant speakers suspended high above the floor. Jack wondered how the cars could take the abuse – front ends were raised six feet before crashing down, and a few of the cars turned over, one of them nearly hitting its owner, who had to drop his controls and scuttle out of the way. The crowd whistled and chanted in Spanish and flashed hand gestures, especially when the winning car was selected and its owner handed his trophy by two women in halter tops and hot pants, who turned and waved at the hooting crowd as the winner drove out of the hall with a blast of exhaust.

Finn pointed at a sign announcing a bikini contest. 'Got to check out the *chicas*!'

'It's on at eight o'clock. Besides, they wouldn't let us in.'

'Wouldn't let *you* in, cracker.'

'If you say so.'

Outside the event centre a steady rain fell, and the sidewalk was thronged with patrons sheltering beneath the marquee. Traders worked the crowd, hawking baseball caps and costume jewellery, and taco and soft-drink stands lined the curb in front of the honking, slow-moving traffic. A graffiti artist had spread a square of old canvas on the ground and was spray-painting gang symbols in bright colours.

Jack pushed through the crowd to the taxi rank. The waiting line was half a block long, and there wasn't a cab in sight.

'Why don't you call your mum?' Finn said over Jack's shoulder.

'She's at the fundraiser until seven. And she puts her phone on silent when she's at these things.'

They watched the graffiti artist for a while. The taxi line grew longer and Jack grew nervous.

'We better try downtown,' he said.

Getting soaked, they walked up 4th Avenue, past the train station and towards City Hall Park. Jack knew this part of town pretty well – his dad's tennis club was in this neighbourhood, as well as the baseball stadium – but as they passed South Washington he grew confused. Construction had closed 4th to all traffic, and big orange signs directed pedestrians east, away from downtown. The rain had thickened. They walked another block and came to a fork in the road. Jack chose to go left, thinking the street would loop back to Yesler Way or Terrace Lane, but it meandered before ending up in a dead end near Route 5. Half-obscured by the misty rain, the traffic swept past them on the wet freeway with a sound like bacon frying. Jack paused, looking left, right and back the way they came.

'You're lost, aren't you?' Finn said.

'Give me a minute – I'll figure it out.'

But the panic in his stomach made him even more uncertain. The rain fell in sheets. He was wet and uncomfortable, and it was already five-thirty. His mom was going to be mad.

'We don't have a choice,' Finn said, moving off. 'We have to go back.'

'Wait up.'

As they arrived back at the fork, a half dozen heavy-looking Hispanic kids approached. Though they were young – only a year or two older than Jack and Finn – they had tattoos all over their arms, and one kid even had them on his neck, so dense you couldn't see any bare skin. They wore Lakers basketball jerseys and gold chains and the standard hats and jeans. Two of them wore red bandannas. They moved with purpose, maybe because of the rain, and Jack kept his eyes on the ground, focused on getting past them without trouble.

Then Finn flashed the sign.

It was a subtle gesture: a downward movement of his left hand, the index finger forming a circle with the thumb, the other fingers spread wide against his shirt. The kids didn't notice it at first. But Finn dipped a shoulder and swivelled in their direction, and the guy at the front, with all the neck tattoos, held up his hand so that the group came to a sudden stop.

'Wass up?' Finn said, and Jack nearly pooped his pants.

The lead guy thrust his head forward. 'Wass *up*?'

'Yeah,' Finn said, his head bobbing in zealous imitation of the leader.

'We're kind of not supposed to be here,' Jack said. His voice was squeaky. 'Just trying to get to City Hall.'

He pointed lamely at the orange signs. Though only a block away, they felt impossibly distant. The five other gang kids – and there was no mistaking what they were –

had fanned out behind the chief, blocking the road.

'Shit. Wass up with *you*, *guero*?'

Beside these guys, Finn was paler and reedier and goofier than ever, the seams of his black cap pearled with raindrops, his red T-shirt soaked through and hanging on his slender frame as if on a scarecrow. The drooping pants completed an effect opposite to the one he intended – he looked like a little kid wearing clothes that didn't fit.

'Just kickin' it,' he said.

This response generated some laughter from the foot soldiers, but the boss's face held its nasty sneer, the veins in his tattooed neck standing out like highway lines on a road-map. Sixteen, maybe seventeen years old, he had a wispy goatee and a chunky medallion the size of a silver dollar suspended at his breastbone. 'Wha's with the sign, buster?' he said. 'You some punk-ass *sureño*?'

Finn shook his head, confused. The guy lifted his hand, extending three fingers in the same way Finn had, but with something menacing and sarcastic in the spread.

Finn still hadn't tuned into the danger. It was as if he was in a video game. 'Just stackin', bro',' he said. 'Walkin' the walk and talkin' the talk.'

These words came out, in spite of their gang rhythm, in a pronounced Irish accent, and the leader couldn't help cracking a smile. The others laughed more loudly.

'Check it out, *esé*,' the chief said to his mates. 'The *vato* goin' all *cholo* on us. He think he one of *us*.'

Further laughter. Emboldened, Finn lifted his left arm and waved it rapper style, fingers configured in yet another sign. The boys at the back, loose now, egged him on.

'*Que pasa, niño?*'

'Sign the little-dick up.'

'*Ese tío está loco.*'

But the leader had noticed something. He stepped forward, the medallion bouncing on his chest, and grabbed Finn's arm. Rotating it so that the bare underside faced upwards, he examined the scarred symbol.

'What we got here?'

'Pachuco cross,' Finn said.

'Say what?'

'My crazy life.'

The leader dropped the arm and squinted at him while removing a pack of menthol cigarettes from his pocket. Slowly, he took a smoke from the pack and stuck it in his mouth. 'You want one?' he said to Finn, holding out the pack.

'No.'

The rain had let up. The chief lit up with the click of a brass Zippo and blew smoke into the light breeze.

'Where you from?' he said to Finn.

'Ireland.'

'*Irish?* Shit. Micks and spics. We blood brothers, *hermano. Comprende?*'

This easy tone frightened Jack even more than the aggression, but Finn lapped it up, nodding vigorously, swinging his arms, showing off his scar.

The chief looked Jack's way and noticed the bandaged wrist. 'Your friend here do the same, right?'

Finn frowned, unhappy with the comparison. 'He just cut himself is all.'

'You Irish into self-mutilation?'

The guy pronounced the last word slowly, syllable by syllable. His mates were restless, and for the first time Jack had the sense they were going to get away unscathed.

'Right,' the chief said before Finn could answer. He stepped back, tugging at the bill of his cap. 'You know Denny Park? The playfield?'

Finn looked at Jack. 'Yeah,' Jack admitted, 'I know where it is.'

'You want to walk the walk, *vato*? Come down Denny Playfield tomorrow. Or any day. Hang out. We got some Irish there.'

'For sure,' Finn said. 'Solid.'

But the chief had moved off, the gang falling in behind him with the chink of jewellery and the shuffle of untied sneakers.

'*Adios!*' the chief shouted.

Finn watched him as if he were Jesus. Without looking around, the tattooed man flicked his cigarette butt over his shoulder so that it completed a high arc and fell in a puddle at the boys' feet, extinguishing with a hiss.

7.

Jack's dad arrived home on Sunday morning. He had flown in on the red-eye from New York and was not in a good mood. Just as Clare had her Irish catch-phrases, Howard had a bag of sayings that summed up how he was. He liked to trot them out when he was tired or annoyed, in a preachy voice that suggested he hadn't said them a million times before: 'I have an excellent sense of direction.' 'You don't have to tell me anything twice.' 'I can't sleep on planes.'

After he had gone to bed for a few hours, Howard watched a news programme while Jack read the Sunday comics and Clare worked in the garden. Finn had returned to bed after delivering papers and was still asleep. When the show was over, Howard clicked off the television and asked Jack to come into his study.

'How's the hand?'

'OK.'

'You got stitches, right?'

'Four.'

'When do they come out?'

'They don't. They're the kind that melt away after a while.'

'Absorbable.'

'I guess.'

Howard sat on the edge of his desk chair, elbows on his

knees. His left eye was bloodshot and he was unshaven. Jack was wary. It was hard to know what his dad would say when he was jetlagged.

'Your mother says you boys were fighting.'

'We weren't fighting. Wrestling. Just goofing around and I tripped. It was an accident.'

'And then you were home late yesterday, soaked to the bone. From the city.' Jack didn't reply. 'I go away for a week and all hell breaks loose.'

'We couldn't get a cab. And anyway, I didn't want to go to that stupid show. Mom made me.'

His dad swivelled in his chair and looked at his laptop, which was open to his e-mail. He launched a file and appeared to be reading, but he turned suddenly and said, 'I count on you to be responsible.'

His tone struck a warning. 'I know,' Jack said.

'Finn has no father at home. He doesn't have your advantages and he doesn't have your brains. I expect you to show some leadership here, and if there's anything you can't handle you let me know. Understood?'

'Yes.'

'Your mom's enrolled the two of you in the camp at the Art Institute.'

'*What?*'

'It's a very good programme, two weeks, and there's a shuttle bus that goes from West Bellevue at seven a.m. Starts tomorrow.'

'When did this happen? She didn't say anything to me.'

'It doesn't matter. You're both going.'

'I hate art.'

'The two of you need some structure. And what about all that model-building you do?'

'I don't anymore.'

But he had returned to his laptop.

'Dad.'

'It's final. Go get ready for the barbecue. I have to do e-mail.'

Every year Jimmy Choi's parents had a barbecue on the last Sunday in June, when they cooked Korean style and invited neighbours to meet their extended family. The food was always good – short ribs, spicy pork, marinated chicken – but Jack felt awkward because Jimmy was a year older and, even though he was a nice kid, his friends were a pain.

Howard wanted to go early and leave early, so they were the first family to arrive. Mr. Choi led them to the living room, which was only used on special occasions. The room was decorated with folding screens, lacquered boxes and jade carvings. The furniture was dark and highly polished and low to the floor. At the end of the room, Mr. Choi's parents sat on rosewood chairs, dressed in what looked like pyjamas. Old Mr. Choi's eyes were slits, and he sat so still that Jack thought he might be asleep. But when Jack and his parents were introduced, as they were every year, one at a time and in order of their place in the family, ending with Finn, the two old people smiled and bobbed their heads and spoke softly in Korean to their son.

'Your boys are growing up to be very fine young men,' Mr. Choi translated.

'Finn is from Ireland,' his dad said, his voice booming in the low-ceilinged room. 'He's Clare's sister's boy.'

More smiles and nodding. Jimmy and his dad wore summer suits and his mom a blue dress with a lotus blossom print. Though he told the story every year, Mr. Choi repeated how his parents had come from Seoul in 1954, penniless, and started a small grocery on Denny Way that was now a chain of seven specialty food stores in northwest Washington. He himself, he added, had attended Western Washington University on a scholarship and was now a human resources manager for Boeing.

After about fifteen minutes of these formalities, the boys retreated to the back yard.

'They do the same thing every year,' Jimmy said defensively. He loosened his necktie and looked at the overcast sky. The day was warm and humid.

'If your grandparents have been here for so long,' Finn said, 'how come they can't speak English?'

'Of course they can speak English. This is just the thing they do on this day. It's a tradition.'

Finn did not look convinced.

'Who else is coming over?' Jack asked.

'My cousins. And Brandon and Zach and Jeff Honecker. And some girls.'

'Who?'

'You don't know them.'

Jimmy's back yard had a trampoline, a brick barbecue

and, at the very back, beneath the overhanging branches of a willow tree, a wooden Buddhist shrine. The family was not religious, Jimmy's mother said every year. She called the shrine a 'cultural artefact'. Beside the barbecue was a trolley with utensils and plates of covered food. The fire smouldered and the air was dense with the smell of burning charcoal.

'Is your mum Korean as well?' Finn asked.

'Fourth generation. Her ancestors came to Hawaii to work on a pineapple plantation, like a hundred years ago.'

Soon, the doorbell was ringing every few minutes as the other guests arrived. Jimmy's friends gathered around the trampoline, drinking soda and making fun of his suit. The boys he'd mentioned were there, as well as Danny Smoltz and Darren Lopez. They were all in Jimmy's class at Bellevue High, where Jack was going in September. Some girls were there, too. Jack didn't know them, but he was pretty sure one was Zach's sister. They wore make-up and earrings and plaid shorts or pastel mini-dresses over black leggings. They looked at each other and laughed a lot, though Jack had no idea what they found so funny.

Mr. Choi came over with a bowl of lettuce leaves and a plate of grilled boneless ribs. He explained to the kids how to wrap a leaf around the meat to make a little sandwich. They each ate a couple.

'These are *so* good, John.'

'Thank you, Megan. Wait'll you taste the *banchan*.'

Jimmy's dad's name was Hae-Jong, but everyone called him John. Everyone, that is, except Jack, who was forced by his parents to call him Mr. Choi. Megan smiled that bogus smile that girls her age used on adults.

As soon as John returned to the grill, she said, 'This stuff is gross. How do you eat it every day?'

'We don't,' Jimmy said. 'It's just for special occasions.'

'Hey Choi,' Brandon said, 'tell your dad to get some hot dogs going.'

'You tell him.'

'They have hot dogs in Ireland?' Brandon said to Finn. It was the first acknowledgement that Finn or Jack were even present.

'You're from *Ireland*?' Zach's sister said. 'Wow. I've never been outside the state of Washington.'

'They don't have hot dogs there,' Zach said. 'They eat Lucky Charms for breakfast, lunch and dinner.'

'Shut up, you goon,' his sister said. But she was laughing.

'They're magically delicious!' Zach said, hopping about like a cartoon leprechaun.

Megan was looking at Jack. 'You go to Chinook?'

'I did. I'm starting in Bellevue in September.'

'Oh, a *freshman*,' she said, eyes rolling.

Jack could have pointed out that she had been a freshman up to a month ago, but he knew that, for her, that was already ancient history.

'Jack builds models,' Jimmy said. 'Has them in a glass cabinet in his room.'

When Jimmy's friends were around, his tone with Jack developed a sarcastic edge.

'Is that what they're teaching at Chinook these days?' Megan said. 'How to build models?'

'I used to build them. I don't anymore.'

'What happened to your wrist?' Danny said.

'I got four stitches.'

'You on suicide watch or something?' Zach said.

'Oh *God*,' his sister said, and she and Megan went to look at the shrine.

The boys bounced on the trampoline for a while and then had some chicken and Korean salads. Jimmy's uncle set up card tables on the patio, and the older relatives gathered to play. The cards had pictures of flowers on them, and during the game players slapped the cards hard on the tabletop and shouted in sharp monosyllables. Mr. Choi took his boyhood kite from the garage, another yearly ritual, and showed it to the younger cousins. For a while it looked as if it might rain, but the clouds lightened and at times the sun peeped through.

The boys started a game of wiffle ball. Finn didn't want to play, but without him there was an odd number, so he reluctantly joined. Jack told Finn that the game was like rounders, but when it was his turn to bat he had no idea where to face or what to do.

'He swings like a girl,' Zach said just loud enough for all to hear.

'C'mon, Xbox,' Brandon said. 'You're in the real world now.'

He struck out every time he was up, couldn't catch the ball and didn't know where to throw when he did get it.

The girls, who watched from the sidelines, shouted deliberately confusing instructions and laughed when he messed up.

When the game was over, Mrs. Choi brought out a tray of cold drinks. The kids went quiet as they drank.

Zach belched and wiped his mouth and looked at Finn, whose face was blotchy and sweaty. He wore his usual outfit and hadn't taken off his knit cap. Zach said, 'Is black the only colour they wear in Ireland?'

Finn stared at him. Megan sniggered in the silence.

'How did you know?' Finn said at last. He looked at Jack. 'Did you tell him?'

'No.'

'Tell me what?'

'They passed a law,' Finn said. 'In Ireland, last year. Anybody who wears anything except black or white can be fined. Even priests and nuns, but that doesn't really matter with them since they only wear black and white anyway.'

'Is this a joke?' Zach's sister said.

'No way. The government copied it from a law you have right here in the States.'

'What law is that?' Jimmy said.

'You know – the one that says that anyone wearing flowery shorts and flip-flops is a wanker.'

He dumped the ice from his glass at Zach's feet and moved away. Jack waited for a moment and then followed.

Behind him, Megan said, 'Isn't that a swear word?'

That night Jack and Finn packed their bags for the art camp: pens and pencils, lunchbox, bottled water, spare

T-shirt. The Institute would provide the art materials, and they'd be doing drawing and mixed media and public mosaic art. They had searched the programme online and it looked really hard. The kind of classes real art students took.

There would be no lie-in after the paper route, so Clare made them go to bed at ten sharp. They lay in their bunks, unable to sleep.

'How are you going to draw with your hand?' Finn said. His voice floated in the darkened room.

'It's my left.'

The barbecue was still going on next door, and they could hear the murmur of voices and the occasional slap and shout from the card game.

'That school … don't know how you're going to stick it.'

'The art school?'

'No. High school.'

'I don't have a choice.'

Finn shifted in his bed, and the slats beneath his mattress creaked.

'They're not all like that, you know,' Jack said. 'The kids in my class are OK. Some of them.'

'Gobshites,' Finn said. 'The lot of them. You know what that means?'

'I can guess.'

The darkness pressed in on them like cotton wool. The curtained window was outlined with the faintest trace of streetlight.

'No gaming in the morning anyhow,' Finn said.

More murmuring from next door.

'Fuckin' gobshites,' Jack said, trying to put on a Dublin accent.

A pause, a rustle and Finn hung his head over the side of the bunk. 'Is that meant to sound like me?'

With his head upside-down, it was hard to tell his expression.

'I don't know.'

Finn laughed wildly, his hair hanging down in limp strands.

8.

The Art Institute was a granite and glass building on the waterfront, overlooking Elliot Bay. The camp kicked off with a meeting on the fourth floor, in a messy room with long, paint-stained trestle tables, deep ceramic sinks and huge picture windows. As the head counsellor introduced the programme, Jack watched taxis and limos pull up to the Edgewater Hotel. Beyond the hotel was the grey slab of the bay, daubed with sailboats, barges and ferries approaching from Victoria and Bainbridge Island. Further still, the ragged mountain peaks of the Olympic Peninsula bulked dull and massive in the mist.

The other kids in the camp were around his age. They were artsy types with blue or scarlet streaks in their hair and clothes like Finn's: oversized black dress shirts, drain-pipe denims and hats – berets, knit beanies, navy watch caps. The kind of kids who liked bands nobody had heard of, read Japanese comics and ate sushi for lunch.

But they were friendly – or those who sat near Jack and Finn were, anyhow. One girl, Chelsea, had been to Ireland with her parents over the summer and was showing off all she knew to Finn, but in a way that wasn't stuck up. Another kid, Joel, lived beside the tennis club Jack's dad belonged to. He claimed he had seen Jack before, though Jack didn't recognise him. They had been to the art camp the year before and knew what to expect.

'Whatever you make,' Joel said, 'they'll say it's great. Put a lump of garbage on a piece of cardboard and they'll say you're the next Andy Warhol.'

'Who's Andy Warhol?' Finn said.

They told them which teachers would give out hall passes without questioning them and how to get into the student cafeteria, where there was free iced tea and soda. Mobile phones were not allowed, but there were payphones in the basement. And if there was a class you didn't like, you could get out of it by claiming you were allergic to acrylic paint or mosaic glue.

'Why would someone who was allergic to paint want to come to an art camp?' Finn asked.

Chelsea raised her eyebrows. 'You think any of us *wants* to be here?'

Best of all, they said, campers got an hour and a half for lunch.

'That's so the teachers can go home and get high,' Joel said. 'And we can go anywhere we want. They let you. As long as we're back by one-thirty.'

'We brought our lunch,' Jack said.

'So let's go to the park. It's, like, four blocks away.'

After orientation, they were given a tour of the building, followed by a loud, confusing hour when smocks, paints, brushes and other materials were distributed. The campers were herded into groups of ten or so and sent to classrooms on the third floor. Finn, Jack and Joel were in the same class. There was only time for one session before lunch, and after the teacher had introduced herself she gave the students pads of paper and graphite sticks and told them to draw a feature of the world around them. Jack sat by the window and tried to sketch the bay and the distant peninsula. The result was crude and childish. He looked over at Finn's pad; he had drawn a perfect charcoal version of the logo from *Gang Feud 3*.

At lunchtime the three boys walked to the park in bright sunshine, stopping at a Minimart on Vine Street to buy a soda. At Denny Way, the street was cordoned off for a road race, and motorcycle cops zipped past, followed by thin, pale runners in sunglasses, with bib numbers pinned to their shorts. The boys had to wait ten minutes before they could cross the street.

At the entrance to the park was a wooden sign that said:

Friends of Denny Park Welcome You
Respect the Park Environment
Ballgames Prohibited Except in Playfield

Finn read the sign. 'The playfield. Where's that?'

Joel pointed at a basketball court behind the trees. 'Over there.'

'Jack – *Denny Playfield*.'

'So?'

Finn rolled his shoulders and made a gang sign. 'That's where those *cholos* told us to come.'

'*Cholos?*' Joel said.

'Yeah,' Finn said. 'Gangsters.'

'We ran into some gang kids last week,' Jack said. 'At the lowrider show.'

'You guys went to a lowrider show?'

'They told us to come down to Denny Playfield to hang out,' Finn said. 'Any time.'

Joel stared at him. 'Are you out of your mind? You know what they do over there?'

'Doin' their thing.'

'Yes, doing their thing. Doing their thing *selling dope*.'

Finn wasn't listening. Gangsta rap was playing in his head, and he swung his arms and thrust his chin forward and crumpled his face into an aggressive urban frown. 'Got to check this scene *out*.'

'Finn, let's just sit down and eat our lunch.'

'Jack, they *invited* us.'

Swaying from side to side, he headed towards the basketball court, his bottle of soda sticking out of the back pocket of his jeans.

'Is he crazy?' Joel said.

'I'll talk to him.'

'Good luck.'

Jack followed Finn. Joel wasn't going anywhere.

The basketball court was flush with the street and surrounded by a chain-link fence. A game was in progress, and all the players were black or Latino. Behind the court was a wide grassy area with picnic tables and large green garbage cans chained to the ground. There was a lot of litter. Clusters of young people gathered at the tables and a few drifted back and forth from these groups to a dark grove of trees bordering the playfield. Competing boomboxes blasted out Chicano rap and reggaeton. There were plenty of NBA jerseys and silver chains and trucker caps, and most of the boys (and some of the girls) had tattoos. There were hardly any white people.

'Finn,' Jack said, 'wait up.'

Finn had let his jeans fall low on his hips and pulled up the sleeves of his shirt so that his scar showed. He swayed in gangsta rhythm, swigging from his soda and surveying the scene like a prison guard. He was starting to attract attention.

'Let's go back.'

'Chelsea said we have an hour and a half,' Finn said.

'Let's go back to the park.'

'What's wrong with here?'

'What are we going to do – eat our lunch at one of the picnic tables?'

'Why not?'

'Because they're full of guys who might beat the crap out of us, that's why.'

'They might beat the crap out of *you*.'

'Well, isn't that a good enough reason?'

Two boys had risen from the closest table and were approaching. Heavily tattooed, they wore tight T-shirts, bandannas and Timberland shoes.

'C'mon, Finn. This is no good.'

One of the boys said, 'You *gabachos* lookin' to cop?'

Jack had no idea what that meant, but he knew what to say.

'No, we're not.'

Finn made a funny laughing sound and stepped towards

the pair. They tensed as he spread his arms. 'You said come down, we down.'

'You what?'

'You told us. Any time, you said.'

As the taller guy peered at Finn, Jack recognised him: he was the leader of the gang they had met on the day of the show. The one with the little goatee and tattoos covering his neck.

His face lit up in a smile. 'Yo, Irish. My man.'

He greeted Finn with a ghetto handshake and spoke to his friend in Spanish, pointing at the symbol on Finn's arm. He looked at Jack. 'How's the hand, bro?'

'Getting better, thank you.'

Finn made a face at Jack's polite language but the guy kept smiling as he checked out Jack's clothes: green jersey polo shirt, cargo shorts, and canvas slip-on shoes. 'You come from the country club, *guero*?'

Jack shrugged.

'Tha's cool. We all democracy down here. Don't judge no book by its cover.'

'We're at art camp,' Finn said. 'At the Institute. We came down here to check things out and eat our lunch.'

Feeling foolish, Jack held up the sealed plastic container that held the cookies and tuna sandwiches his mom had made for them that morning.

'Come on over,' the kid said. 'We eatin' Mickey D's.'

A half dozen other kids were at the table, younger than the leader, including two girls. The tabletop was littered with McDonald's food bags, Styrofoam containers, hamburger wrappers and paper cups. Some of the kids were smoking, but there was no evidence that Jack could see of any drugs. After some talk in Spanish, the leader introduced himself as Ramón and circled the table, pointing at each of his friends and pronouncing the name or nickname of each with a flourish. Jack caught 'Benny D' and 'Carina', one of the girls. Jack and Finn introduced themselves, though Finn pronounced his name 'Feen'. While they ate their sandwiches, the others went back to their Spanish conversation, though Carina kept glancing at Jack.

When they had finished, Ramón flicked his cigarette onto the grass and lifted a boombox to the tabletop. 'You Irish know Daddy Yankee?'

'Yeah,' Finn said.

'So, who is he?'

Finn shrugged and Ramón laughed. He punched some buttons on the boombox and turned it up loud. The song, 'Gasolina', was sneering rap, in Spanish, with synthesised beats and Latin rhythms. Two of the guys got up and mimed in sync. When a woman singer cut across the male vocal with the chorus, '*Dame más gasolina*', the two girls at the table sang along, bobbing their heads and pointing at the boys before clutching each other and laughing. Finn jumped up and joined in the dancing.

When the song was over, one of the kids asked Finn about his scar, and he held out his arm so they could examine his claim to fame. While the boys leaned in for a look, Carina came around the table and sat beside Jack.

Up close, she was younger than he had thought at first,

close to his own age. She had dark eyes and very white, even teeth. She wore tiny silver earrings and, around her neck, a silver cross, which shone brightly against her brown skin.

'Your friend,' she said, 'he is so funny.'

'He's my cousin.'

'Ah. You are both Irish.'

'He's *really* Irish. He lives in Ireland, and he's visiting for the summer. I live here in Seattle.'

'I am from Puerto Rico.'

He nodded. She wore a red halter top, a denim skirt and a charm bracelet around her wrist with tiny pink hearts and a gold number 15.

'You like the music?' she said.

'It's OK.'

'You know who is *La Gata Gangster*?'

'No.'

'The girl on this song. Her name is Glory. Daddy Yankee is good, but for me she is the real star.'

'I never heard of her.'

'Never? Where you been living?'

She laughed and touched his arm.

'Is she like Catwoman?' Jack said.

'Why?'

'*La gata*. That means cat, right?'

'*Hablas español!*'

'I studied a little in eighth grade. I'm going take it as my language in high school.'

'I will be careful what I say. You know, Glory is from

Santurce, same *barrio* as my family. And Benicio del Toro. *Estrella de cine.*'

'Movie star,' he said.

'*Muy bien!*'

While Jack and Carina spoke, kids streamed back and forth from the grove of trees, whispering to Ramón and waiting for a response. Some of the kids looked about ten years old, miniature versions of the big boys. Ramón would nod in one direction or another and they would head off, scuffing the dirt with their sneakers. He was clapping and moving in time with the music, but he was also alertly scanning the playfield from one corner to another.

'Where do you go to school?' Jack said.

'I start at Westside in September. And you?'

'Bellevue.'

She whistled. '*Niño rico.*'

'My family's just ordinary.'

'Oh?'

Jack nodded at Ramón. 'What's he looking for?'

She frowned. '*La policía.* Sometimes they come, they tell us we are … you know, that we cannot be here. Here there are tables, here we are having lunch. Just like you, rich boy from Bellevue.'

'I told you, I'm not rich.'

'*Claro,*' she said sarcastically, but she was smiling with her eyes.

When it was time to go, Jack had a tough time getting Finn to leave. Everything he said and did seemed to entertain the gang kids, and as they walked away Finn waved his arms, flashing signs and shouting random phrases he had picked up from the video game while his audience hooted in response.

'*Feen!*'

It was Carina calling him and motioning. He ran back and they spoke for a moment.

'What did she want?' Jack said when they were finally on their way.

'What do you think she wanted?'

'I don't know.'

'She thinks you're *caliente*.'

Jack glanced back. Carina waved. 'C'mon,' he said gruffly. 'We have to get back to class.'

9.

Jack's parents went out for dinner that evening. It was something they always did the night after his dad returned from a trip. The restaurant was local, so they left the boys on their own. Up to now, Jack's aunt had always come over. The word 'babysit' had never been used, but that's what it had been.

As they were leaving, Howard said, 'Did you tell him about the tour?'

'Oh,' Jack's mom said, 'the high school rang. There's a tour of the school in the morning. For the new freshman class.'

'What about the camp?'

'You can miss one day. Finn, you can go as well. It will be interesting for you to see an American high school.'

'I'd rather go to art camp.'

His parents glanced at each other.

'You don't mind going on your own?'

'Sure, I can get the bus like we did this morning. The camp is brilliant.'

His mom had that look on her face she got when Jack gave her the impression she'd been right about something all along. 'Well, isn't that great. We thought you'd like it. I suppose you two can do without each other's company for eight hours.'

His dad winked as he closed the front door. 'Behave yourselves, boys.'

As the car pulled out of the driveway, Jack said, 'You love art camp, huh?'

Finn pointed at the computer. '*That's* art. Will you get me a bowl of cereal?'

When he returned with two bowls of Fruit Loops, Finn was running *Gang Feud 3*. Though something was different.

Jack watched over his shoulder. 'Is that the demo?'

'Yeah.'

'No it's not.' The disc-drive light was blinking. 'You got the real game.'

'So what?'

'Where'd you get it?'

'What difference does it make? Watch this.'

Onscreen, one of the characters from the demo drove a lowrider Impala through a ramshackle neighbourhood. The street corners were crowded with gang kids who shouted at the car as it passed. It pulled up to a house and the man got out. Jack realised that Finn was using the controls to manipulate the character. The man carried a baseball bat and a brown paper bag.

'What's in the house?' Jack said.

'I'm making a delivery.'

'Of drugs?'

Finn snorted. 'What do you think?'

Jack set the bowls of cereal on the desk. The man climbed the porch steps and knocked on the door with the bat. Another man opened the door.

'*Tienes cocaína?*' the other man said.

'*Sí.*'

'*Me siguen.*'

Finn's character did as he was told and followed the man into the house, which had the same lay-out as the one in the demo. They passed through two rooms and in the third room two guys jumped from behind a door and ambushed him. Finn's fingers flew across the keyboard as the man onscreen beat off the two attackers with the baseball bat. When they fell back, he took a pistol from his waistband and shot them both. Blood spattered everywhere. The man who had let him in ran away and Finn chased him through the house, cornered him in a bathroom and shot him. His body fell into the bath and blood dripped down the white tiled walls.

Sirens howled and blue lights flashed in the windows. *Get out, get out!* Jack thought, but Finn's character went deeper into the house until he came to a room with a safe. Finn punched more keys and his character pulled out a stick of dynamite and blew open the safe. Inside was a briefcase. It was full of money. He put the paper bag in the case, closed it and made his way back to the front door.

Jack heard the crackle of a police radio. 'Careful,' he said.

Finn edged open the door and through the gap they saw a policeman on the sidewalk, hands on his hips, looking up and down the street. Behind him was his squad car, its blue light swivelling in the night. Finn had his man take aim.

'What are you doing?' Jack said. 'It's a cop.'

'It's either him or me.'

Finn's man shot twice and the cop fell into the gutter. The man ran out, jumped in his car and drove away. The car careened down the street, hitting pedestrians and other cars as more sirens wailed in the distance.

Suddenly the action stopped and the screen blinked with rows of statistics. Finn wiped his palms on his T-shirt and exhaled.

'Finished the level,' he said.

'Wow.'

Finn took the bowl of cereal onto his lap, ate a spoon-ful, and grinned. 'Amazing, huh?'

'It's a whole new world.'

Jack's mom dropped him off at the high school at nine the next morning. Above the entrance was a hand-painted banner in blue and gold lettering that said: WELCOME BHS CLASS OF 2012. Beneath it, teachers and seniors with name tags greeted the new students as they arrived and ushered them to separate classrooms according to the first letter of their last name. Jack met some of his eighth-grade class-mates from his middle school, Chinook, and there was much chatter and laughter and a buzz of excitement at coming to a place that felt so grown up.

Twenty kids were in Jack's room, including Cody Fisher and Jason Kramer from Chinook. Cody's dad also worked at Microsoft. Their tour leader was a math teacher, Mrs. Schilling, who asked them to be quiet and said she had a sore throat. After a few hoarse remarks, she led them through the hallways where they saw the lockers they would be assigned and the foyer where they examined the trophy cases and honour-roll lists and a collage of photographs of former students now serving in the military. They also visited the library, music room, science labs, theatre hall, cafeteria and the office of the school newspaper. They criss-crossed other groups, and there was a lot of squealing and hooting as students greeted friends in the other tours.

By eleven they had been herded into the gym, where they sat with their groups and waited for the principal to address them. The babble of their voices echoed in the big space. The hardwood floor was polished to a high sheen, the fixtures were spotless and the glass basketball backboards glinted. On the wall at the south end of the gym was a giant, professionally painted mural of a roaring wolverine, the school's mascot. More banners hung from the rafters. On each was printed a single word in capital letters: RESPONSIBILITY, INTEGRITY, DIVERSITY, COMMUNITY, RESPECT.

The principal was a tight-lipped woman with straight hair that hung from her head like a curtain. She was the kind of woman who could make two hundred kids shut up just by staring at them, and when there was total silence she introduced herself as Mrs. Lawson. She did not have a sore throat. In her booming voice she said that each and every one of them would be getting to know her very well over the coming four years. She said that Bellevue High was ranked in the top hundred high schools in America and that anyone who attended was privileged.

'And with privilege,' she said, 'comes…'

She slowly lifted her hand and pointed at the banner that read: RESPONSIBILITY.

Nobody said a word. Like Jack, they knew where this was going. She spoke for another twenty minutes, pointing at each big word in turn. She finished by saying that they were going to work hard and have a lot of fun at the Home of the Wolverines.

As the kids filed out of the gym, each was handed an information pack and two helium-filled balloons, one blue and one gold. They toured the school grounds and sports facilities and ended up on the football field, where the school band had assembled. In the open air, their good-natured rowdiness returned. Some had lost their balloons, but most still had them as they formed a semicircle on the fifty-yard line and a teacher rang the school's 'spirit bell' from the archway at the end of the stadium. The band played the school song and the teacher told the kids to release the balloons, which drifted in the light breeze and filled the sky with the school colours as the new kids whistled and cheered.

After lunch, Jack was cutting the grass when his mom told him there was a phone call for him. She smiled in an odd way.

'*Hola, amigo. Cómo estás?*

'Who's this?' Jack said.

'Who you think? Carina.'

'Oh, hi.'

He was on the kitchen extension. His mom was on the deck, pruning her plants. He wasn't sure if she could hear him.

'How'd you get my telephone number?' he said.

'That was your *mamá*?'

'Yes.'

'*Muy simpática.*'

Behind her voice were shouts of a basketball game and rhythms of a boombox. He pictured her at the playfield on her mobile phone, away from the picnic table, leaning against the chain-link fence.

'I had to go to my high school this morning. We had a tour.'

'Yes. Feen told me.'

'He was there today?'

'He is here now. That boy, he sure like to dance and sing the reggaeton.'

The kitchen clock said half past two. Finn should have been back at art camp an hour ago.

'Does he know you're calling me?'

'No. Is my secret.'

The music and yelling and Spanish in the background sounded very strange to him as he sat at the kitchen table and watched his mom through the window. He could hear the clock tick. His parents had installed a new kitchen last winter, with a granite-topped island in the centre, a giant fridge-freezer and a full set of French copper pots suspended from a ceiling rack.

'I was sad when Feen come today and you were not here,' she said.

'Well, like I said, I had to go to the high school.'

'Will I see you *mañana*?'

'I don't know.'

'Feen said you will be here tomorrow. For sure.'

'Maybe. But we can't be cutting camp. We'll get in trouble.'

'So come at lunchtime. Ramón, he buy McDonald's, every day. Big Mac. Filet o' Fish.'

'Yeah. OK.'

After the call he went straight back to mowing the lawn. As he emptied the grass-catcher onto his mom's compost heap behind the shed, she came over and pretended she was putting away her shears.

'Who was that on the phone?'

'This girl I met.'

'Oh?'

He brushed cut grass from his shirt.

'Is she foreign?' she asked.

'She's an exchange student from Puerto Rico. I met her on the tour this morning. Part of the whole thing about studying Spanish. You know, the language option?'

His mom reached out and put her hands on his shoulders, as if she wanted to hug him but couldn't finish the gesture. She still wore her gardening gloves. *You're growing up so fast*, the look on her face said. It was the look she got when she had discovered something about him that had actually changed a long time ago.

'Oh, Jack. This is such an exciting stage in your life.'

'I guess,' he said and walked back to the lawnmower.

10.

After dinner, Finn announced that he wanted to show the family his artwork from the camp. Jack cleared the dishes and Finn dealt onto the tabletop half a dozen playing-card-sized sketches of tattoos, drawn in red and navy blue ink on stiff tablet paper: the word MEGADETH in gothic script, a grinning skull smoking a cigarette, a pair of teardrops, an array of stars and hearts and a wheel of the zodiac. The sixth and last one was Jesus on the cross, which made his mom exclaim, 'Oh!'

Nobody said anything for a minute.

'What class was this in?' his dad said.

'Freestyle.'

'Sounds like an excuse to do anything you want.'

'It's about self-expression.'

'Looks to me like the doodles kids do in school when they're bored.'

'*Howard*,' his mom said. 'I think they're very good, Finn. There's real talent there.'

Jack's dad, whose back had been bothering him since his trip, arched and frowned. 'Talent is all about how you apply it,' he said and went off to his study.

'Don't mind him,' she said. 'He's not feeling the best.'

Finn gathered up the drawings and thrust them back in their folder.

'Listen,' she said, 'why don't we go to the mall to buy

Jack's school clothes? We can get some ice-cream after-wards.'

'I don't need any school clothes.'

'Of course you do.'

The information pack from the school tour included clothing guidelines. Students were not allowed to wear torn jeans, body jewellery or any item of clothing with sexually explicit language on it. Gang-affiliated clothing was also banned. But nothing said kids had to wear chinos and collared shirts, which Jack's dad said he had to wear.

Jack had shown his parents the guidelines. His dad wouldn't budge. The issue, he said, was 'non-negotiable'.

'It's called "business casual". It says you're relaxed but serious about your work. You can still wear sneakers or whatever.'

'Sneakers look stupid with chinos,' Jack said.

'I don't agree.'

Of course he didn't agree because that was what he wore himself. But Jack didn't see why that meant *he* had to wear them.

In the car, his mom tried to make him feel better. 'Finn has to wear a uniform to his school, isn't that right, Finn?'

Finn didn't answer. He'd gone into zombie mode after the comment about his drawings and was listening to his iPod whilst staring out the window and rubbing the scar on his arm. All he did was rub that scar.

'Didn't stop him from getting suspended.'

His mom looked at him in the rear-view mirror. Jack had forgotten this was something he wasn't supposed to know. Though he could say that Finn had told him.

The mall was deserted and depressing, with the bad music sounding even worse in the emptiness and random clumps of slack-jawed, glazed-eyed teenagers drifting in the retail glare. Jack stubbornly said he wanted to go to American Eagle or Abercrombie and Fitch, but his mom insisted on Macy's, which had the right range of brands for his dad's personal dress code.

Jack knew that his mom's patience was running thin, but he couldn't bring himself to humour her. This whole outing was ridiculous. Inside the store she stopped at the make-up counter and told the boys to go to the Ralph Lauren section.

Finn ran his hand through the rack of polo shirts and laughed. 'You be lookin' fly wearing these. They'll *love* you down at the playfield.'

'So you're the expert on the playfield now.'

'Better than hanging out in a shite shop like this.'

'Or going to the camp?'

'I went to the camp.'

'All day?'

Finn sneered. 'So Carina rang you.'

'How do you know?'

'Because I gave her your number, you gobshite.'

'Yeah, well, cutting class is exactly what's going to get us both in trouble. They'll call my parents and I'll get blamed as usual.'

Finn frowned with mock pity. 'Poor you. But just so you know, I didn't miss anything I wasn't meant to. I told them I was allergic to glue and they let me off.'

Jack stalked off and went through the motions of

examining the chinos. Rack after rack of pants and they all looked dorky. Finn followed him over. A saleswoman approached and asked if they needed any help, and when Jack said no she slid slowly back to the register, eyeing them suspiciously.

'I showed my drawings to Ramón,' Finn said. 'He thought they were cool. He said they're as good as what the real lads do.'

'He would know.'

'They were asking for you. Carina told me to make sure you come to lunch tomorrow. Said they'd buy us whatever we want from McDonald's.'

Jack took a beige pair from the rack. 'My dad expects me to wear *these*. I mean ...'

'He just wants you to look like him.'

'Please.'

'The black ones aren't so bad.'

'Would *you* buy them?'

Jack felt the material. The price tag said eighty-nine dollars. He wouldn't wear these if you *paid* him eighty-nine dollars.

'Is Carina ... why is she involved with those guys?'

'What do you mean "involved"?' Finn said. 'She's their friend.'

'She doesn't seem like the type to hang around with gang kids.'

'Ramón said he'd bring me to a tattoo parlour tomorrow.'

'I just don't want us to get in trouble. Bad enough that Carina called the house.'

'It's not her fault your parents won't let you get a mobile.'

'I get one in September.'

'Yeah. Like the laptop.'

The saleswoman had circled close, straightening racks and glaring at them. When Jack's mom arrived, brisk and irritated, the woman backed off.

'All right,' she said, 'what have you picked out?'

'Nothing.'

'Nothing?'

She looked at Finn. He shrugged.

'Fine,' she said. 'But we're not leaving here until you have your school clothes. That's final.'

She was sounding more like his dad all the time. Jack looked away from her, down the long aisles of merchandise, so colourful, so glittery, so fake.

At home, Jack's mom told him to spread his new clothes across the sofa so his dad could see what they'd bought.

'I'll put them away.'

'Dad will be delighted. Show him.'

Jack flung the bags onto the sofa. 'There. He can open them himself if he wants to.'

Stiff and wide-eyed, Finn nodded to suggest that Jack should turn around. His dad stood in the doorway. He had pushed his reading glasses to the top of his head, and his eyes had that blurred look they got when he'd been working on his computer for a long time.

'You don't like the things your mother bought you?' he said.

'They're all right.'

'Because you can always buy your own clothes if that's what you want.'

'I said they're OK.'

'And everything else I work hard to get for you. Your bike and your surf board and the television and the trips we take you on and – '

'All right, Howard,' his mom said. 'He understands.'

His dad's face was dark and lumpy. 'I don't think he does. I'm in there' – he gestured vaguely towards his study – 'working overtime, trying to make a living to pay for all this stuff he seems so put out to have to use. I'm seeing code samples so off the mark, Clare … you don't want to know.'

'Why don't you go back to work.'

'And here I am being made to feel like an ogre for wanting to buy my son decent clothes for school. Don't you think there's something backwards there? Jack, I'm talking to you.'

'I'm listening.'

'I don't think you are. Don't you think there's something mistaken about this attitude of yours?'

Before Jack could answer, the phone rang.

His dad answered. 'Oh, hi … Yes, yes, he's doing great … Not at all, I'm just taking a break … Yes, we love having him here. Getting on gangbusters.' He put his hand over the receiver and said to Finn, 'It's your mom.' He nodded. 'Yeah, sure, Orla … OK … Well, why don't you tell her?'

He removed the receiver from his ear. Finn reached

for it, but Jack's dad said, 'She wants to talk to Clare.'

He handed the receiver to Jack's mom and told Jack to collect his shopping bags. He brought the boys into the kitchen.

'She won't be long, Finn. Sisters, right?'

He looked confused, as if he couldn't remember why he was annoyed. Glancing at the living-room door, he told Jack to put the clothes away and to stop complaining and think about his behaviour.

In the bedroom, Finn said, 'Jaysus, I thought he was going to go mental there for a minute.'

'I wonder what your mom wants.'

'Speaking of mental.'

Jack took the tags off his new clothes and hung them up while Finn sat on the edge of the bunk. They heard Jack's dad rearranging chairs in the kitchen. A lawnmower was going outside. After a while Clare stuck her head in and said, too brightly, 'Your mum wants to talk to you, Finn.'

It was the first time Jack had heard her say 'mum'.

While Finn took the call in the kitchen, Jack stayed in his room and opened the door a crack so he could hear his parents. They spoke in low tones, and he had to strain to hear them.

'I told her she shouldn't tell him,' his mom said, 'but she feels he has to know.'

'That's because she doesn't have to deal with him right now.'

'Don't be unfair. She misses him.'

'Like a hole in the head.'

'Shh.'

'He can't hear us. He's talking.'

'He'll probably be fine about it. I can't see how it could come as a surprise after what he did.'

'Then what was the whole point of sending him over here?'

'Why are you being so aggressive?'

'I'm not being aggressive. I'm under pressure. Kilroy will want this report in the morning and the code's all over the place. You have no idea.'

'Then go do it. And by the way, I think this whole experience has been great for him. For Finn. It's Jack who's difficult at the moment.'

'Has it occurred to you that maybe Jack's acting up because the kid's here? I mean, did you see those drawings? I'd like to get a shrink's opinion on those.'

There was a long pause.

'What could he be telling her?' his dad said.

'It's the first time they've spoken since the day after he got here.'

'Probably said more to her on this one call than he has to us the whole time.'

'Do you know what she asked me? If we were bringing him to mass.'

'She still goes to mass?'

'I don't know.'

'Well, don't get any ideas. Sundays are manic enough around here.'

The living-room door opened. Finn said something

that Jack didn't catch and then came in and went straight to bed. He didn't say a word until the lights were out.

'They're not letting me go back to school.'

'Any school?'

'The one I was in up to now.'

'Why?'

'Don't pretend you don't know.'

'Because of the thing on your arm?'

'Yeah, that. And calling the principal a spare prick.' He laughed in the darkness. 'I'm glad. I hate him and I hate that kip.'

Beneath the crickets came the faint sound of music. Something Oriental. Probably Mr. Choi playing traditional Korean music while he cleaned his garage.

'You know what he said to me? The principal? That I was an embarrassment to my mother. Doesn't give a shite about me; he only cares about his snobby school and the tossers on the rugby team.'

'Is your mom mad?'

'She's mad, so she is. Mad as a hatter.'

The music had stopped. The crickets were suddenly very loud.

'Finn?'

'What?'

'What class did you get off? You know … because you're allergic to glue.'

'Mosaic.'

'Right after lunch?'

'Yeah.'

A car roared past, its headlights flashing across the ceiling of the bedroom.

'I think I'll have a Big Mac,' Jack said. 'With fries.'

'Oh, yeah.'

11.

After their McDonald's feast, Ramón took Finn and Jack to The Mighty Quinn tattoo parlour near the science-fiction museum. Carina came with them. The place was empty when they walked in, but a huge man with a pony-tail, a goatee and a wide grin came out from the back, and he and Ramón went through a complicated ritual of hugs and handshakes and Spanish phrases.

'You know the sweet Carina.'

'*Cómo estás*, cookie?'

Carina smiled. She had her hair tied back with a blue ribbon, which matched her top. Her forehead was smooth and round and her eyes looked even larger than usual.

'And these be the Irish I'm telling you about,' Ramón said, 'come down Denny to see a real *varrio*, yeah?'

The big man stroked his beard. His eyebrows were wild and woolly and every square inch of visible skin, except for his face, was tattooed. A trail of silver studs, each smaller than the next, ran from the wing of his nose to the corner of his mouth.

'You know what "Quinn" means in the Irish language?' he asked. His voice was high-pitched for such a big guy. '"Chief". That's right. My ancestors were warrior kings who kept Ireland free from invaders for a thousand years. You can look it up. Let me show you something.'

He led them to a showcase of tattoo stencils. The top shelf was dedicated to Celtic designs: crosses, knots, spirals, shamrocks. There were trees and animals and letters of the alphabet, each drawn with squiggles and curls that reminded Jack of St. Patrick's Day.

'This is our speciality,' Quinn said. 'People want a tattoo that says "Hey, I'm Irish," this is where they come. We understand the heritage and the style.'

He put a hand on Finn's shoulder. 'What's your name, kid?'

'Finn.'

'You're shittin' me.'

Quinn looked at Ramón.

'What I tell you, huh? Real Irish.'

He pulled Finn over to a metal chest and took out a folder. 'We keep the best stuff under lock and key. Have a look.'

While Jack peered over his shoulder, Finn leafed through the folder, page after page of tattoo templates of Celtic heroes, their names written beneath each drawing in the same curly script: Cormac, Oisín, Medb, Diarmaid and Gráinne, Conán.

When he came to Fionn Mac Cumhaill, Quinn leaned across and tapped the drawing with his forefinger. 'There he is. The great one. *May your heart grow bolder like an ironclad brigade.*'

'I spell it without the "o",' Finn said.

'Then you spell it wrong. This is the man who caught the salmon of knowledge. Who built the Giant's Causeway. Who could walk on water. They teach that over there, right?'

'Not really.'

'Then you have to learn it. It's your heritage. Your name. When the fire-breathing fairies lulled the men of Tara asleep at harvest time so they could burn down the king's palace, Fionn stayed awake by stabbing himself with his own spear. Then he killed the fairy leader. He was like the Spartans. Like Ulysses. The greatest of all heroes.'

'How much for one of these?' Finn asked.

'For a full-on tattoo? Two hundred per character. Plus tax. But for a real Irishman like you I might be able to cut a deal.'

During this conversation Carina had leaned close to Jack so she could see the drawings. He felt the soft skin of her arm against his own, breathed her sweet, lemony scent. With her hair pulled back he could see her silver earring and a delicate swirl of downy hair, like a Celtic spiral, beneath her temple.

Quinn gave them a tour. The showroom had counters lined with stools where customers could examine the books of stencils. The walls held framed photographs of past work and the shelves trophies from competitions. Out back was an air-conditioned studio with leather seats like barber chairs and a long worktop covered with the tools of the trade: tattoo machines, latex gloves, needle sets, ink trays. Everything was as clean as Jack's mom's kitchen. Lunchtimes were quiet, Quinn said, but business was booming. Irish tattoos were hot. He gave them each a stencil of a Celtic symbol and a can of salve, which he said was good for any sore, not just fresh tattoos. He had Ramón lift his shirt to show them the latest work he'd done for him: a five-point star between his shoulder blades, coloured and striped like the Puerto Rican flag.

'See?' Quinn said. 'The dude's proud of where he's from.'

'*Puerto Rico siempre*,' Ramón said.

'You guys should be, too.'

'I am,' Finn said and pointed his thumb at Jack. 'But he's from Bellevue.'

On the way back to the playfield, Ramón and Finn stopped to inspect a motorcycle, and Jack and Carina walked ahead. Along Denny Way, people ate lunch in outdoor cafes, music blared from car radios and a light breeze fluttered the flags and bunting that shops and restaurants had hung for the Fourth of July. Carina kept close to him, and he was aware of the glint of her gathered hair in the sunlight and the sidelong glow of her bare shoulder.

'So, now you want a tattoo?' she said.

'I don't think so.'

'Feen does.'

'Finn doesn't really think things through.'

'No?'

'A tattoo is forever. It's not something you do just because you feel like it all of a sudden.'

Also, though he didn't say it to Carina, if he got a tattoo his dad would kill him.

'You don't believe in forever?' she said.

'What – like dying and going to heaven?'

She shrugged and smiled, as if the question she'd asked was really about something else.

'I mean, what if you're, like, forty,' he said, 'and you

have kids and stuff and there's this big skull or whatever on your arm that you can never get off?'

He was talking more than usual and saying things that he really didn't mean.

'You think about when you are forty?' she said.

'Not really. But I can't see my dad with a tattoo.'

'My father has two. No, three.'

It had not occurred to him that she had a father. Though it seemed stupid for him not to have thought of it.

'What does your dad do?'

'He work for the Parks Department.'

'Does he come down to the playfield?'

She laughed. 'No.'

They passed over the entrance to the Battery Street Tunnel. An ambulance flew down Highway 99 and its siren went suddenly silent as it disappeared into the underpass.

'Jack, you know something?'

It was the first time she had said his name. The 'J' came out funny, but it sounded smooth and musical.

'What?'

'I have a tattoo.'

'You do?'

'*Claro.*'

'Where?'

'You want to see it?'

His throat was tight and his mouth dry. Did she have to ask him that?

'I guess,' he said.

She took his hand and led him down an alley and into a doorway, its smooth concrete apron running a few feet to a metal door, like the exit for a movie theatre. She turned and leaned against the door and pushed the left strap of her halter top to the side, revealing a small tattoo of a bird with a black head and striped wings and a circle of orange around its neck.

'That's cool,' he said.

'A tanager. *Pájaro national*. The bird of Puerto Rico.'

'Right.'

'Touch it.'

She leaned close to him and he laid a trembling finger on the tattoo, which was on the soft rise of skin between her collarbone and her breast. He felt the beating of her heart. She closed her eyes and bent her face to his and it was the most natural thing in the world for him to kiss her. She pressed into the kiss, from underneath, and he grew dizzy, the doorway and alley and the tall buildings above swirling about his head as he returned the moist push of her lips.

Out of breath, he pulled back. His own heart pounded. She drew her lips in and smiled. '*Besas bien*,' she whispered.

'What does that mean?'

'Ask your teacher.'

'Will it get me in trouble?'

'You never know.'

Getting through his art classes that afternoon wasn't easy. No matter what he was assigned, Jack wanted to draw a picture of Carina. But he knew he wasn't able, so instead he wrote her name on the art tablet, over and over, until he realised that he wasn't sure how it was spelled. Did it begin with a 'C' or a 'K'? He thought 'K', but he would have to ask her to be sure. And what was her last name? Maybe he could go down to the payphone at the next break and call her.

She had given him her mobile-phone number on a slip of paper. The row of numerals, written in purple ink in her curved handwriting, was like a tattoo of her presence, and he took the paper from his wallet every few minutes and gazed at it. When he recalled the tingling smoothness of her skin and the soft push of her lips against his own, his throat thickened and his head felt dizzy, as if he wasn't getting enough air.

Finn knew something was up. At break he said to Jack, 'I told you she likes you.'

'She's friendly.'

'No – she *likes* you. Where did you two go, anyway?'

'Nowhere. We went back to the playfield.'

'You were holding hands.'

'No, we weren't.'

'I don't think the lads are too thrilled about it. Benny D and the boys.'

'Shut *up*. It's none of your business. Or theirs.'

'Tell that to *them*.'

Jack's parents had been invited to a party that night in Redmond, but at the last minute his mom said she didn't feel well, so they stayed at home. Jack had planned to call Carina, and their decision filled him with a panic he had to work hard not to show. Finn wasn't happy either. He had been denied a perfect opportunity to play *Gang Feud*, and he grew sullen.

At the dinner table, his dad said, 'What are you two so quiet about?'

When neither answered, his mom said, 'They're tired. Up at half four to do their route, then camp all day. You boys need to be getting to bed earlier. Enough of this ten o'clock nonsense.'

'*I'm* not tired,' Finn said.

'You know how depressing it is to go to bed when it's still light out?' Jack said.

'One more day,' his dad said. 'Tomorrow's Thursday and then you have the long weekend.'

Friday was the Fourth of July, so there was no camp. A few days ago, Jack had longed for the holiday. Now he dreaded it. His mom had made pizza, his favourite dinner, but he had no appetite. As he forced himself to eat, he waited for the phone to ring, scared it would but even more scared it wouldn't.

After further silence, Finn blurted out, 'My mum said I could get a tattoo.'

Jack's dad took a sip of beer and wiped his mouth with his napkin. 'She did, did she? When was that?'

'On the phone last night.'

His mom said, 'Are you sure, Finn? That doesn't sound like Orla.'

'We could give her a call,' his dad said. 'Just to make sure.'

'You don't have to ring her. She told me I could. She

said that if I'd got one before, I mightn't have done this to myself.'

He raised his arm and displayed his scar. Jack saw that his parents weren't sure whether Finn was making this up.

'How's *your* hand?' his mom said to Jack, trying to change the subject. The bandage had been removed and the stitches dissolved.

'Fine,' Jack said, without raising his hand from under the table.

'She said it was OK,' Finn persisted. 'Last night.'

'How could you afford it?' she said. 'Those things must cost a lot of money.'

'Doesn't matter how much they cost,' his dad said. 'He's not getting one. Not as long as he's staying in this house.'

Howard sat perfectly still, both hands on the table. The bubbles rising in his beer glass were the only movement. Finn stared at his plate and rubbed his scar. Was this the moment when he would lose it and call Jack's dad a gobshite or a spare prick? Would he shout about the playfield and the tattoo parlour and ruin everything? But he stayed quiet.

They finished dinner and cleaned up and his dad went to his study to work for the evening. His mom took gardening tools from the shed and Jack spooned food for the cat into a bowl. Finn stood at the open sliding door, one foot over the threshold, tapping the glass with a coin.

She returned to the deck with a trowel and an empty flowerpot, and Finn said to her, 'Did Jack tell you what he's been learning?'

'No.'

'Spanish.'

Jack felt blood rise to his face. He didn't look up.

'At art camp?' she said. She sounded confused.

'You could say he has, like, a real tongue for the language.'

He pocketed the coin and went inside.

'What did he mean by that?'

'I have no idea,' Jack said.

12.

Thursday morning was never-ending. First there was a problem with the route. Jack's drop was a paper short, so he had to write a note to a customer and phone the circulation department to request a late delivery. Then he and Finn nearly missed the camp bus, which was pulling out of the shopping-centre parking lot in West Bellevue as they arrived. They sprinted along the access road to flag it down, and Finn tripped on a speed bump and tore his pants. Finally, there was a boring three-hour pottery class with a crazy woman with long grey hair and Mexican jewellery who kept shouting, 'Centre! Open! Floor!' as the kids took turns at the potter's wheel. Their hands got filthy, and the lines at the sinks were long, so it was nearly twelve-thirty by the time they had cleaned up and headed out to the playfield.

The closer Jack came to seeing Carina, the more the world around him became a mystery. Walking up Denny Way was like floating in a bubble. A thin rain fell from low cloud, and the top of the Space Needle was invisible. The fronts of buildings and the gaps of sky between them merged in a blur of grey. In the gutters, linden and cottonwood leaves floated towards the storm drains like tiny rafts. Passing cars had their lights on, and the faces of pedestrians were obscured by hats and umbrellas. It was like being in a movie or a dream, and the only sound was the growing thunder of his heartbeat.

From a distance they sensed something different about

the playfield. The basketball court was empty and the picnic tables unoccupied. Unfamiliar figures moved in the mist. As they approached, these figures took shape: several policemen and a crew of city maintenance workers in green bib overalls. A squad car had driven across the field and close to the grove of trees, its rooftop lights flashing white and blue. The workers were spearing trash and dismantling the tables. A flatbed truck trailed them slowly, and two of the men were stacking table parts on the back of it.

Finn said, 'The enemy.'

He hopped from one foot to the other and rolled his shoulders. But Jack felt strangely calm. He wondered if one of the park workers was Carina's dad. Most of them looked Hispanic. 'What happened?' he said.

'What do you think?'

'Why don't I call Carina's cell?'

They found a payphone in the lobby of the Best Western hotel across the street, but when Jack called he got voicemail, in Spanish. He didn't leave a message.

'Do you think they were arrested?'

Finn scoffed. 'Ramón told me about this. It happens, like, every few months. They wait for a while and the cops get bored watching them and everything, like, goes back to normal.'

'So what now?'

'I'm hungry.'

They bought hamburgers at McDonald's, and when they came out Finn turned right on 9th Avenue, in the opposite direction to the Art Institute. Jack asked him where he was going.

'When this happens they go to Bobby Morris.'

'What's that?'

'Another park.'

'C'mon, Finn.'

'It's not that far.'

'How do you even know about it?'

'I know.'

'We should get back.'

'Don't you want to see Carina?'

Just hearing her name spoken was exciting. If he didn't see her this afternoon, it would be four days.

'She'll be there?'

'Where else?'

As Jack followed Finn, his stomach knotted up again, but he wasn't sure if it was because of Carina or the trouble they'd be in for being late.

The Bobby Morris Playfield was a lot bigger than the Denny, with tennis courts, a soccer pitch, two baseball diamonds and a basketball court. Beside it was a tidy park with a water fountain and a reflecting pool and a wide area of well-tended lawn. There were no tables, but in spite of the weather, students from the community college and a few mothers with young children were gathered around the pool eating lunch.

Jack didn't see any gang kids.

'What makes you think they're here?' he said to Finn.

'You think they'd be hanging in broad daylight? With the cops nosing around? Follow me.'

In the far corner of the park, under the cover of trees,

was a triangle of bushes surrounded by a low wall. Sitting along the wall were some of Ramón's boys, including Benny D and two guys nicknamed Caballo and Bárbaro. Carina wasn't there, and neither was Ramón.

Finn moved down the wall with his hand up, receiving high fives and pretending he could understand the Spanish banter. Jack held back. The party atmosphere of Denny was missing: there was no boombox, no food, no laughter. The boys were sullen, especially Caballo, who sat on the end of the wall, smoking a cigarette and staring at Jack. He was thin and pale, with a shaved head and clothes so large they looked comical. He had a tattoo of a horse's head on his upper arm.

'Yo, *guero*,' he said to Jack. '*Quieres?*'

He thrust the lit cigarette, pinched between thumb and forefinger, in Jack's direction.

'No thanks.'

Caballo spoke rapidly in Spanish. The others laughed.

'No smoke, huh? *Majo niño.*'

More laughter. Jack wondered what *majo* meant. Though the laughter told him it was probably better not to understand.

Caballo's attention drifted, but Bárbaro hopped down from the wall and walked up to Jack. He wore a trucker cap so low that Jack couldn't see his eyes.

'You looking for someone *in particular*?' He smiled and glanced at the other boys, as if showing off this English phrase.

'Is Carina around?'

'Ah. *Careeena*,' he said, mocking Jack's accent.

Bárbaro was short and heavily muscled. Probably a year or two older than Jack. He stood close, smelling of aftershave and cigarette smoke. When Jack stepped back, he stepped forward. Jack looked over the boy's shoulder at Finn, who watched the situation warily.

'Feen,' Bárbaro said, staring at the ground, 'what you think? One of us is Carina?'

Finn laughed nervously. Was he scared? Jack imagined that his own fear was obvious, like a stain on his pants.

Bárbaro had a wispy moustache, which arched like a caterpillar when he sneered. 'She a sweet little piece for you, no?'

'No. She's a friend.'

'Ah, friend. *Su amiga.*'

'Yes.'

Bárbaro tilted his head back so that Jack could see the intensity of his eyes, which were small and dark and angry. There was also wildness in them. Jack had thought that Ramón was the fiercest, most aggressive of the gang, but now he saw that he was the one who kept the aggression under control.

Caballo got up from the wall and stood beside Bárbaro. He had lit a fresh cigarette and waved it under Jack's nose. 'What you want with this *chica*? What I *think* you want?'

'I don't want anything.'

Caballo poked Jack in the chest with the lit end of the cigarette. Sparks and ash showered down his shirt and there was smell of burnt fabric. It was a new T-shirt, with Japanese lettering and a picture of Homer Simpson. He had bought it himself because he thought it was cool.

Finn shouted, 'Lads, check this out!'

He swung his hips and moved his shoulders up and down, clicking a reggaeton beat with his tongue and bobbing his head. He was awkward but funny, and Benny D laughed. Caballo and Bárbaro turned to watch.

'*Uno, dos, tres,*' he shouted, thrusting an arm in the air and breaking into a full-on Daddy Yankee impression, bending his knees and dipping his body as he swept his hands across his face and sang:

> *A ella le gusta la gasolina*
> *Dame mas gasolina!*
> *Como le encanta la gasolina*
> *Dame mas gasolina!*

His pronunciation was good, but his skinny frame jerked like a puppet. Everyone was laughing now, even Jack, and Benny D lined up beside Finn and joined in the groove as the other boys clapped in time and shouted out the chorus.

Without missing a beat, Finn caught Jack's eye and made a little motion with his chin. *Go*, it said. *Go now.*

'Jack!'

Across the street, behind a dense stream of traffic, Carina was walking sideways and waving. It was like a movie scene where a boy and girl longing for each other are separated by an impassable barrier. But there was a gap almost immediately and she ran across the road, her gait graceful and smooth, her hair bouncing on her shoulders.

She wore ballet shoes, white legging jeans and a black leather jacket over a white camisole. Her lips glistened like flower petals and her eyes had been widened and deepened with mascara and shadow. A small silver cross hung from her neck on the thinnest of chains. She looked so much more grown up than the first time he had met her.

'There you are,' she said, stepping onto the sidewalk. 'I didn't think I see you today.'

He moved towards her instinctively but pulled back at the last moment. The intensity of her presence and the style of her clothes and make-up made him shy.

'I called you,' he said.

'I lose my phone. During the raid.'

The raid. It was a moment before he realised that she was talking about the police at the playfield.

'Is everything OK?'

She smiled and flopped her hand. 'This happen all the time. *Los credos*, Ramón call them.'

'*Los credos?*'

'Pigs.'

'Ah.'

Tiny beads of moisture had collected in the wave of hair above her forehead and glistened as she moved her head.

'You come back?' she said.

'Where?'

'Bobby Morris. Our new hangout.'

She brushed her hand against his and a jolt of energy

ran through his body. He remembered their kiss of the day before and how wonderful he'd felt afterwards. But there was also a coldness in his mind that he didn't understand, and he was confused that such opposite feelings could move within him at the same time.

'I have to get back,' he said. 'I'm already late.'

'But Feen is there.'

He shrugged. 'That's Finn. I guess he doesn't care.'

'Please. Come.'

'I don't think those guys like me.'

'Who?'

'Caballo. The others.'

'Forget about them. You stay with me.'

'I have to get back,' he repeated.

She frowned, as if he had passed his confusion on to her. 'Maybe we meet tomorrow?'

'My parents have plans for the holiday.'

'So, Saturday.'

The need to put her off upset him. 'Look, you don't know what it's like with them. I can't just say I'm going into the city, you know, and disappear or get the bus or whatever. There isn't even a bus. I'd have to tell them I need a ride and they ask me where I'm going and who I'm meeting and how I'm getting home. And what do I say?'

Instead of making this silly speech, he wanted to hold her hand, examine her tattoo, kiss her again. But it was as if his words and actions were being controlled by something outside of himself.

She stepped back and pressed her lips together. 'You tell them that you see your friend.'

'It's not as simple as that.'

A passing car honked, making them both jump. She pushed her hair behind her ear. 'So, I see you next week.'

'Why don't I call you tomorrow?'

'I tell you – no phone. But I call you.'

'OK,' he said slowly. 'But listen – if one of my parents answers and they start asking you any questions, tell them you're an exchange student. At Bellevue High.'

'Why?'

'Just do.'

She became stiff and distant, like the popular girls in school who pretended he didn't exist even when he stood right in front of them.

He continued: 'It's just that – '

'That you have shame of me?'

'No. Of course not.'

'Then what?'

Her large, dark eyes flashed with anger.

'You don't understand,' he said.

'No. I don't understand. Maybe next week you explain.' She walked away.

'Carina.'

'I see you on Monday,' she said without turning around.

The short stretch of sidewalk between them was like a canyon. He turned and walked back to camp.

13.

Jack's family had a Fourth of July routine. His dad would rise early for a round of golf at Rainier Country Club. When he got home he made a pancake breakfast for the family and afterwards they cycled to Downtown Park in Bellevue to watch the parade and listen to the live music. In the afternoon, he grilled Omaha steaks and Polynesian pork chops. Jack's Aunt Sandy and her family arrived with three salads (one red, one white, one blue), strawberry shortcake, and a quarter barrel of Chicago root beer. If the Mariners were playing an afternoon game, they watched it on television. When the relatives had left, Jack and his parents drove into the city to view the fireworks from the waterfront.

Up to now, the Fourth had been Jack's favourite day of the summer. But this year was different. He was tired and nervous. He had slept poorly, replaying the conversation with Carina over and over in his head. He wondered why he had been so cold towards her and why he had told her to pretend she was from Bellevue High. It was a stupid thing to say. He didn't expect her to call but hoped she would, even if his parents should answer the phone. Otherwise he would have to wait until Monday to say he was sorry, and that seemed like years away.

But in another way, Monday felt as if it would come too quickly. He did not want to face Caballo and Bárbaro again, even with Ramón there. But how else could he see Carina?

'What did they say when I left?' he'd asked Finn last night, when they were both in their bunks.

'Nothing.'

'Nothing at all?'

'They were messing. They're sound, they really are.'

'The one guy poked me in the chest with his cigarette. He could have burned me.'

'It was all play-acting.'

'I don't think so.'

'Don't be such a baby.'

'Will Ramón be there on Monday? Are they going to be back at Denny Playfield?'

'Jays', you're all questions tonight, aren't you?'

The parade was led by the Grand Marshal, a sergeant major in the Washington National Guard. He was followed by forty new citizens from seventeen countries who had been sworn in that morning by a US District Court judge. His mom had gone through the same ceremony seven years ago, though she hadn't walked in a parade. There were soldiers home from Iraq in army combat uniform, majorettes twirling batons and the marching band from the high school; an old hook-and-ladder fire truck, a long line of Cadillac and Lincoln Continental convertibles and a beer wagon drawn by Clydesdale horses; floats with Irish dancers, a jazz band, a beauty queen and her runners-up and girls from the Swedish Cultural Centre in long, colourful skirts with aprons, bodices and bonnets, throwing candy to the kids along the route.

None of it had any appeal for Jack. He couldn't believe he'd ever found this spectacle interesting. And Finn wasn't exactly excited. He slouched with his hands in his pockets, staring disdainfully at the marching soldiers and policemen and listening to Chicano rap and hip-hop on his iPod.

Afterwards they walked around the park. Every event was designed for someone really young or really old.

'You guys want to go to the Fun Zone?' his dad said.

'*Dad*. It's for kids.'

'You went last year.'

'Yeah. And it was boring.'

A country and western band played on the main stage. There were sack races and hula-hoop competitions and a pavilion with booths for local businesses and charities, including Bellevue Animal Rescue, where his mom had volunteered for an hour. They said hello to her, petted a few stray cats and left the pavilion.

Howard squinted into the sun and strapped on his cycling helmet, which made him look goofier than ever. 'Well, if you guys refuse to have fun I don't see any point in hanging around here.'

It didn't get any better at home. Sandy and her husband, Jeff, and Jack's cousins Kyle and Amanda arrived early in their SUV with their dog, Ranger, who went crazy in the back yard and chased the cat up a tree.

Jack's dad and Aunt Sandy bickered.

'But you never bring the dog.'

'I told you I was going to.'

'No you didn't.'

'What?' Sandy said. 'He's supposed to stay chained up at home? He can't have fun?'

'At the expense of the cat? Look at her – she's terrified.'

The cat was on a low branch, her fur spiked, her back arched. Ranger was throwing himself at the tree trunk.

'Don't sweat it, Howie,' Jeff shouted from the deck, beer in hand. 'He'll calm down.'

Jeff wore a Hawaiian shirt, beach pants and sandals. On the peak of his weathered baseball cap was his company's slogan: WE LAY LUMBER. He was the only person who called Jack's dad Howie. He did it especially when he was teasing, and the teasing had an edge to it. At some point in the day he would ask certain questions that he asked every time he came over:

'Just what exactly is it that you *do* at work, Howie?'

'Hey, Howie, you been to Bill Gates's new house yet?'

'Where can I get a pair of shorts like those, Howie? With all the pockets?'

Jack's mom arrived back from her volunteer stint with a tray of cupcakes. She made a show of introducing Finn to his 'cousins'.

'They're not related by blood,' Jack said.

She glowered. 'Well, neither am I. But we're all family.'

She and Sandy laid out the food, helped by seven-year-old Amanda. Amanda's brother, Kyle, was a year younger than Jack. He was a miniature version of his dad: rough around the edges, with the same thick features and hair that fell in front of his eyes.

'Guys,' Jeff said, 'don't leave all the work to the women. Roll in the barrel.'

The boys went out to the SUV to get the keg of root beer. Since their last visit, Jeff had bought a new Chevy Tahoe, with huge tyres and tinted windows and a Play-Station in the back seat.

For the first time that day, Finn perked up. 'This is so cool. Do you have *Gang Feud*?'

'*Gang Feud*, *Call of Duty*, *Rainbow 6*, *Splinter Cell*, *Gears of War*.' Kyle ticked off the names of the games on his fingers. 'You want me to keep going?'

'Can we play?'

'For a few minutes. Otherwise it runs down the battery.'

'You guys,' Jack said, 'we're supposed to bring in the root beer.'

'What's the matter? Think your dad's going to catch us?'

'Those games – they're all rated M.'

Kyle scoffed. 'Yeah, right. Like that means anything. Not everyone's as tight-assed as Howie, you know.'

Jack grew furious. 'Shut *up*, Kyle.'

Kyle stepped away and peered at Jack though strands of hair. 'I'm only joking.'

'Joke about your own dad, you little jerk.'

Jack wrestled the keg from the rear of the SUV. As he carried it into the house he heard Kyle say, 'What's eating him?'

The picnic table on the deck was covered with food: the meat in its marinade, rolls, sauces, pickles, sliced tomatoes and Sandy's salads: red potato, white potato and blueberry coleslaw. Jack's dad fired up the barbecue while Jeff peered over his shoulder. Sandy told a story about a neighbor of theirs who'd been locked out of the house when his wife found out he was cheating on her. Drunk, he had pounded on his front door at three in the morning, pleading to be let in and waking up the whole street. Jack's mom scrunched up her face as if disgusted-interested, but Jack knew the look: she was uncomfortable with the subject matter, especially with Amanda standing beside them, listening to it all. As if Sandy didn't tell a story like this one every time she visited.

He walked to the back of the yard to be by himself and to spare his mom a little embarrassment. Ranger had given up on the cat and lay panting at the base of the tree, his paws crossed in front of him. Ropes of saliva sagged from his lolling tongue to the springy grass beneath his jaw. The cat had disappeared.

Jack stroked the crown of his head. 'Good doggie.'

In the distance a firecracker exploded. Ranger growled. In the farther distance, but not that far, Carina would be celebrating the day with her family. Or did Puerto Ricans celebrate the Fourth? They probably had their own Independence Day. He would have to Google it.

She was probably with Caballo and Bárbaro and the other macho *cholos*.

His stomach felt as if something was gnawing at its lining. He would find it hard to eat and harder to say why he wasn't hungry. *It's a food day*, Sandy would say, *c'mon – eat up*. Kyle would wolf everything down.

On the deck, Jeff watched Jack's dad lift chunks of

steak from the marinade and put them on a platter.

'Hey, Howie – are those *zippers* on your shoes?'

'Why do I bother?'

'He's family.'

'Who needs it? Really. Who needs it?'

They were crossing the floating bridge into the city for the fireworks. The sun had set and the western sky was flaming pink. Howard leaned forward in the driver's seat, thumbs kneading the steering wheel. Clare stared down at the water.

'Since when did this become a tradition? And why? Because she's my only sister? Next year we're not inviting them.'

'That's what you said last year.'

'This time I mean it.' He glanced at the boys in the rear-view mirror. 'I've never seen Jack so miserable.'

'I'm not miserable.'

Finn removed his iPod earbuds and said, 'Kyle's brilliant. When are we going to see him again?'

His mom turned in her seat and smiled. 'You see, Howard? You're overreacting.'

They parked near Qwest Field and walked up Western Avenue towards Waterfront Park. Jack's dad strode ahead. His bare calves and pink polo shirt caught the fading light. Clare had resigned herself to his mood and hung back with the boys, telling them to listen for harbour seals and keeping an eye on Howard so he didn't get lost in the stream of people heading to the park. The lights on the

Space Needle blinked as the evening darkened. The tide was out, the air had grown cool and the smell of the sea was powerful and bracing.

The park was south of the Art Institute and Denny Way but close enough that Jack could not get Carina off his mind. Though she would likely be in her own neighbourhood tonight. They reached the park ahead of the big crowds. They had brought lawn chairs and a cooler full of drinks and snacks, and they settled themselves near the water, beside the entrance to the aquarium, with a good view of the bay.

The fireworks were spectacular. Bellevue had its own display, but the Seattle show was unmatched, with magnificent fountains of colour, sizzling trails of sparks and plumes bursting from plumes that made the crowd gasp and brightened their upturned faces like flashes of lightning. Every time Jack thought the most amazing explosion had happened, an even better one would follow, including a series of red, white and blue cascades that hung in the air like giant palm trees, trailing flares and lighting the sky and outlining Olympic Peninsula so that it looked like a huge black whale.

West Seattle was a mile or so away. As he watched the show of colour and sound he knew that she could see it, too. Wasn't that a connection?

Afterwards they waded through the departing crowd, sluggish from the day's food, sun and spectacle. Howard remained impatient, complaining about the congestion and urging them to walk more quickly so he could get home and get back to work.

As they crossed Madison Street, a voice shouted, '*Feen!*'

Through the blurred flow of bodies – suburban people, most of them, in shorts and running shoes, sundresses and sandals – Jack saw Ramón and his gang, assembled on the street corner as if in a movie poster, tattooed, pierced, draped in chains and basketball jerseys and red bandannas. Jack and Finn had stopped instinctively while his parents kept moving. Ramón led his boys across the street. By the time he reached them, Jack's parents had doubled back.

'Say what, Irish. You down celebratin' the big Yankee *fiesta*?'

Ramón gave Finn a dramatic ghetto handshake and smiled at Jack. 'Your *primo* showin' you a bangin' night?'

Jack's dad had his hands on his hips. 'Do you know these boys?'

'This here Ra*món*,' Finn said in his fake street voice, tilting his head and extending his hand gang-style, the fingers stiff and splayed. The gang kids laughed.

'Is that right? Well, Ramón, I am Howard Klements. Finn is my nephew and Jack here is my son.'

Benny D stood beside Ramón. Caballo was in the ranks behind them, but Bárbaro and Carina were not there.

Ramón took in Jack's dad with a sweep of his eyes. Beside Jack's parents, he looked dark and menacing, though his face held no aggression.

'Yo, Howard, you got a couple of good kids here.'

'I don't need you to tell me that.'

It was as if the whole street went quiet. The guys behind Ramón stirred, but he stood still as a stone, the only movement a tiny quiver of the tuft of hair on his chin. He stared Jack's dad down, his expression unchanged. Small explosions rang in the distance and laughter from the passing crowd filtered into the bubble of tension surrounding the group. Finn watched the face-off as if it were a scene in a video game.

The stirring behind him turned to a grumble. Ramón cut it short with a sharp burst of Spanish, but his eyes stayed fixed on Jack's dad. Finally, he spat in the gutter and smiled at Finn and Jack. '*Adiós, amigos.*'

The gang left in a single movement, like dancers in a music video. Ramón led with a rolling swagger, to the sound of medallions clinking and sneakers scuffing the pavement.

Jack's mom was clutching her husband's arm.

'For God's sake, Howard, what was *that* all about?'

He jiggled the change in his pocket and looked at the boys. 'That's what I want to know.'

14.

On the bus to art camp on Monday morning, Jack said to Finn, 'Can you do something for me?'

'What?'

'Tell Carina to meet me at the Space Needle. At one o'clock.'

'What if I don't see her?'

'You're going down there, aren't you? At lunchtime?'

'Yeah.'

'So you'll see her.'

She hadn't called. All weekend Jack had stayed within earshot of the phone. Every hour or so he checked to make sure there was a dial tone, then panicked, thinking she would call and get a busy signal while he was checking.

Of course, if she did call, his mom or dad might have reached the phone before him. But not hearing from her was worse than the fear of them linking Carina's voice to the incident with Ramón.

His dad had said nothing all weekend about meeting the gang kids. Jack thought he'd forgotten about it, but on Sunday night he called him into his study.

'I might be wrong about this,' he said, 'but those guys seemed more drawn to Finn than to you.'

'I guess.'

'How do you know them?'

'We met them at the lowrider show.'

He shook his head. 'I told your mother that was a bad idea.'

'It's no big deal, Dad. They like Finn. They think his accent is funny.'

'Have you seen them since?'

'Since when?'

'The show.'

'No.'

His dad leaned close. His face was dark with earnestness. 'Listen to me, son. There's their world, and there's ours. I know it isn't politically correct to say this, but the values are very different.'

'You don't know anything about them.'

'Individually, they may be great guys. That kid Ramón, he seemed OK. It's the culture that disturbs me.'

'What's wrong with their culture? They're Puerto Rican.'

'Not their nationality. The drugs and the violence. The gang stuff. That's what I'm worried about. It's part of their world and they're victims of it.'

'They never said anything about drugs to us.'

'Of course not. You only met them once.' He sat up and turned to his laptop, as he always did when he was about to end a conversation with a command. 'You and Finn are forbidden to see them again. Is that understood?'

There was no point arguing.

'Yeah.'

'So tell your cousin. And make sure he understands.'

***

As soon as morning classes had finished, Finn left the Institute. Jack waited twenty minutes and walked to the Space Needle. He had brought his route savings, eighty-five dollars, and his plan was to invite Carina to lunch at the revolving restaurant at the top of the Needle. His dad had taken him there on his twelfth birthday. You could see Mount Rainier from up there, and Mount Baker and the Cascades. And today was a beautiful clear day. The restaurant was the right place to show her how much he liked her and to explain why he didn't want to talk to her with the gang boys listening in.

When she didn't show at one, he circled the base of the tower several times. He was nervous and light-headed and unsure if he could eat, even if she did turn up. After half an hour, he plucked up the courage to go to Denny Playfield. There were no cops, and a basketball game was in progress, but only a sprinkling of the usual crowd were in the field behind the court, which looked strange with the tables and garbage cans removed. The tracks from the Parks Department truck they had seen on Thursday were dried and rutted and cut straight across the sparse grass like a bowling alley.

He had no choice but to continue to Bobby Morris. The people walking along the sidewalks and eating lunch in the sidewalk cafes annoyed him. They talked and laughed and waited at the pedestrian lights as if everything were the same. As if there were no uncertainty in anyone's life.

Of course, a few minutes ago he had imagined he

would be eating lunch with Carina high above the city, laughing and joking, telling her how much she meant to him. But how much could he mean to her if she hadn't even bothered to show?

The playfield was packed. A tennis tournament was on, and spectators leaned against the mesh fence, cheering on one player or another. The children's wading pool was open and a lifeguard in orange swimming trunks paced its edge. Picnickers crowded the grass slopes and a rainbow arched through the spray of the water fountain. Jack walked slowly to the rear of the park, hoping to catch a glimpse of Carina from a distance and beckon her away from the gang. But the little triangle in the corner was empty. By the time he had searched the whole park and nearby side streets, it was after two o'clock, and he was late for the afternoon session at camp.

Finn was not there when he returned. He joined water-colour class and sat beside Joel and Chelsea. The teacher, Mrs. Jankovic, frowned as she handed him his materials and pointed at a cluster of hyacinths in a glass vase on a table at the front of the classroom: purple, red, orange, white and yellow.

This class was their fourth on watercolours, and they were expected to show progress in the second week. With a few apparently random strokes of her brush, Chelsea, who had plans to attend the Institute after high school, had painted a convincing still life in a matter of minutes. Jack stared at his blank sheet, not knowing where to begin.

'Where's your Irish friend?' Joel whispered.

'He's my cousin.'

'Is he cutting class?'

'I don't know.'

'You know what Mr. Lambert said. If he misses an-other class…'

'I know.'

Chelsea leaned close. 'Do an outline.'

'What?' Jack said.

'Remember? In pencil?'

Moving his shoulder so that Joel couldn't see, Jack drew a crude outline of the flowers with an HB pencil. A wash, the next step was a wash. He mixed red paint with water and applied the first layer of colour. It smeared more widely than he intended and, because he'd added too much water, dripped down the page. He dabbed at the run-off with his sleeve, spreading the smear. He ripped the page from the tablet and started over.

'Jack.'

'I'm trying to do this, Joel.'

'You know what's he's doing, don't you? Your cousin.'

'No.'

'Look at me.' Jack stopped drawing. Joel was wide-eyed with his news. 'You're not going to believe this. He's asking people here if they want to buy weed. Asking them at break.'

'He's selling drugs?'

'Not exactly. More like, "If you want it, I know where you can get it."'

'That's not selling anything. It's just him trying to impress people he doesn't know.'

'Doesn't matter what his reasons are. He could get kicked out; the cops could get called. You could get in trouble, too.'

The second pencil outline was worse than the first, but Jack decided it was good enough and mixed more red paint.

'A kid in my school,' Joel said, 'he got caught with, like, ten ecstasy tablets: expelled. No "three strikes and you're out". Just gone. And it gets put on your record.'

'Not enough water,' Chelsea said to Jack.

'Will you *shut up*,' Jack hissed.

Mrs. Jankovic looked up from her desk. Chelsea had covered her mouth with her hand.

'Not you,' Jack said to her. 'Him.'

'*Sorry*,' Joel said, flaring his eyes at Chelsea.

When Jack boarded the bus home at five o'clock, Finn was sitting by himself at the back. Relief spread through his chest like a cold drink.

'Where have you been?'

'Shh.'

'Nobody can hear us.'

'The pigs are watching Ramón's *pandilla*. They have to stay moving.'

Finn chewed gum. His eyes flicked back and forth.

'What, you're speaking Spanish now?' Jack said. 'What's a *pandilla*?'

'What do you think? His gang. They're being persecuted. For who they are.'

'And you're skipping art camp to look after them.'

Finn was jumpy and distracted. He smelled of spearmint and cigarette smoke. Or maybe it was more than cigarettes. Not that Jack would know.

'I went to both playfields,' Jack said.

'We weren't there.'

'I know. Did you see Carina?'

'No.'

For a moment Jack was relieved. She had not ignored his request to see her. But it had now been four days since their awkward moment in the rain. Was something wrong? After all, she had his telephone number.

'Why wasn't she there?'

'She was helping her mother with something. That's what Ramón said.'

'With something? With what?'

'Jesus, Jack, she *wasn't there*. OK?'

The bus lurched forward. The other passengers, a dozen of them or so, sat near the front. As they headed towards Route 5, Finn stared down at the street, as if looking for something. An empty bottle rolled down the aisle and a girl at the front laughed.

Jack pinned the bottle with his foot. 'So instead of going to camp you're out there roaming the 'hood,' he said. 'With Ramón's *pandilla*.'

'Better than that boring art shite.'

'Mr. Lambert called me out of class. He wanted to know where you were.'

'What did you tell him?'

'That you went home sick.'

'Good man.'

'So you think that's all? He probably called my mom. That's what they do here. If you don't have a note they call your house.'

'Is she home today?'

'I don't know. But even if she isn't he'd leave a message. They're not that stupid. My dad's already mad about last night, and if he hears about this he'll go psycho.'

'So? Nothing to do with you.'

In his frustration, Jack grabbed Finn's arm and yanked at it. Finn pushed him away and moved so that there was a row of seats between them.

'The last time you did that you ended up in hospital,' Finn said.

The bus moved swiftly along Route 5, in the shadow of the tall buildings of the business district but above the hustle of the streets. The bright sun glinted off the flowing traffic and the green road signs. Sparks fell from the torch of a welder doing work on the skeletal grid of a new skyscraper. The world kept moving and Jack was going nowhere. Even Finn was in motion – causing trouble, true, but going after something. *You don't understand*, Jack had said to Carina as she walked away. He was the one who didn't understand.

When they arrived at the mall in Bellevue, he stepped from the bus and viewed the shopping plaza as if for the first time: coffee shop, Bed & Bath, furniture dealer, pizza restaurant. Retail outlets as far as you could see: sporting goods, shoes, electronics, clothes, cars. Designed for easy access by the new SUVs and people-carriers the locals liked to drive and landscaped with exotic trees and bark mulch and grass so green and closely trimmed it looked artificial. Not a piece of litter in sight.

As he and Finn unlocked their bikes from the rack beside the petrol station and hitched their schoolbags onto their backs, Jack felt as if he had arrived in one of those perfect suburban towns in the movies, where everything is bright and cheerful and runs like clockwork, but where you can't help feeling that something bad is about to happen.

15.

When they got to the house, no one was home. The red message light on the answering machine was blinking and the digital message counter tallied a glowing *1*.

'Listen to it,' Finn said.

'What if it isn't Mr. Lambert?'

'What if it is?'

Or, Jack thought, what if it's Carina?

The new message had been received at 2.47 p.m.

'Mrs. Klements, this is Chris Lambert, head of summer studies at the Art Institute. I need to confirm that Finn Geraghty went home sick today, as he has not returned to the Institute from his lunch break. Please call me before five p.m.'

He left a number. As they listened, Jack cocked an ear for the sound of car tyres on gravel. The cat meowed at the back door.

'Delete it,' Finn said.

'I don't think so.'

'Go on. What's the point of leaving it for them to hear?'

'Let's tell my mom there was a misunderstanding. Make up some story.'

Finn reached across him and pressed the delete button and the flashing light went dark. Jack felt as if he had been caught shoplifting.

The next morning Finn did not help Jack with the route. He stayed in bed and said from beneath the covers that he wasn't feeling well. But when Jack returned an hour later, he was playing *Gang Feud* and eating a bowl of Cap'n Crunch cereal.

'So, you're not going to camp.'

'Oh, I'm coming.'

'I thought you were sick.'

'Not as bad as I thought.'

'Thanks for sticking me with the whole route.'

'I haven't been paid yet.'

'Really? Neither have I.'

On the way into the city, Finn was even jumpier than he'd been the day before. He wore his gang outfit: the low-slung jeans, death's-head T-shirt and Dodgers baseball cap. Plus a new medallion Jack hadn't seen before, embossed with the image of a rearing horse and suspended on a thick silver chain. He tapped his foot furiously to Chicano rap on his iPod, turned up so loud Jack could hear the lyrics from across the aisle.

Are you selling weed? Jack was tempted to ask. But he said nothing.

As they entered the Institute, Finn tugged Jack's shirt sleeve.

'I have to do something,' he said. 'Tell them I'll be in by second session.'

'Do what?'

He walked away, holding up two fingers. 'Second.'

But he didn't show up for second session. Or the third.

In the mosaic class, the last before lunch, Jack was called to the door. It had to be Mr. Lambert. As he crossed the classroom, he sifted excuses: Finn was still sick, he had an appointment, he'd fallen and hurt his knee. But what was the point? By now the man would have spoken to his mom. The shit was about to hit the fan.

But it was Carina at the door, pale and nervous, moving uneasily from foot to foot and smoothing her hair with the flat of her hand. Her face was puffy, as if she had been crying, and her eyes were lightly bloodshot.

'What is it? What are you doing here?'

'You have to come,' she said. 'Feen is in trouble.'

Jack turned and peered through the small window in the classroom door. The teacher held a square of coloured glass in the air and spoke intently to her students.

'I can't just leave,' he said.

'Please. He is in danger.'

He had no choice. He followed her through the silent hallway, expecting Mr. Lambert or a hall monitor to pop out from a doorway at any moment. A trail of reflected light stretched along the polished floor, from their feet to the exit. They moved along it as if in slow motion. When they reached the double doors and broke through to the bright day outside, the fresh air against Jack's face was like a splash of water.

All weekend Jack had imagined what he would say when he saw her. But her appearance and their quick departure were blurred and breathless, and as she led him briskly down Elliott Avenue, in the opposite direction to the playfields, he felt he had missed his chance to explain. His nerves were in turmoil: there she was, walking alongside him, after all the suspense of not hearing from her. She was dressed plainly, in jeans and a sweatshirt, without make-up or her charm bracelet or other jewellery and with her hair tied in a ponytail. Her simplicity was deeply attractive. She had nothing to hide. She was not out to impress.

But where were they headed?

'Carina, what's going on?'

'Quickly. We talk on the bus.'

They passed beneath the viaduct, alongside the shops and restaurants of Pike Place Market and past the art museum. At Union Street they boarded a number 21 bus. She paid their fares.

They sat and caught their breath. She offered him a weak smile.

'Not too long,' she said. 'It is in High Point.'

'What is?'

'Where we must go.'

Earlier in the summer, two boys had been shot in High Point. One of them had died. The joke among kids he knew was that it been renamed 'Low Point'.

'You said he's in danger.'

'That's all I know. Ramón, he tell me to bring you.'

The sympathy in her eyes gave him hope.

'I missed you,' he said.

'My mama, she is sick. *La gripe.*'

'Flu. So you've been looking after her.'

'Of course.'

'Why didn't you call me?'

'And say I am from Bellevue?'

Her sarcasm stung. 'I'm sorry about that,' he said. 'I shouldn't have said what I said.'

She shrugged and leaned forward so she could see how far they had gone. The bus turned a corner and the low landscape of West Seattle spread before them in the distance.

He touched her arm. She didn't look at him, but she didn't pull back either.

The area wasn't as run-down as Jack expected, but the house Carina led him to was derelict. Plywood boarded the windows and iron grillwork barred the front door. Gang graffiti had been sprayed on the front of the peeling house, and the wooden steps leading to the entrance were gapped and splintered. Broken glass littered the sidewalk, and as they crossed the walkway Carina nudged the larger shards aside with the toe of her sneaker.

She knocked twice, waited for a moment and then knocked three times. The man who let them in was new to Jack: older than the others, with a big belly and a full beard, dressed entirely in black. Though it was dark inside the house, he wore sunglasses. He indicated that Jack should lift his arms, then patted Jack down and took his wallet and keys. He gestured them to follow. In spite of his size he moved lightly, like a cat, and led them to what had probably been the kitchen, though the sink and counters and appliances had been ripped out. The windows here were barred but unglassed and unboarded, and the linoleum floor had long gashes in it. The smell of garbage was overpowering.

In the middle of the room Ramón sat backwards on a kitchen chair, his legs thrust to the sides, his chin resting on the chair-back. Six or seven others stood around him, including Benny D and Caballo and another big guy in black clothes and shades.

No one acknowledged their arrival except Ramón, who stood and offered his hand. Jack shook it, ghetto-style, as best he could. The air of menace was intense, though it seemed clear it was not aimed at him.

'*Tú lo has encontrado*,' Ramón said to Carina.

'*Claro.*'

'Your cousin,' he said to Jack.

'What's happened?'

Ramón shook his head. 'Feen want to do a run. You know, drop some product to some customer.'

'You mean drugs.'

'I ain't saying what. Not the point. But these customer, you know, they get the wrong idea. They think maybe your *primo* worth more than the product. Is other gang, right? So they lookin' for some tribute.'

'What does that mean?'

'*Dinero!* Money, man,' Ramón snapped. 'What you think?' He spread his arms wide, as if to suggest, *What could I do?* Children's voices drifted in from outside. Benny D went to the window and looked into the side yard.

'You sent him with drugs to another gang?' Jack said. A warmth had spread from his chest to his arms and his head. His throat was dry.

'Hey, we no send him nowhere. He *ask*. You know Feen. He talk the talk, now he want walk the walk.'

'So what are you going to do?'

'You mean, what are *we* going to do.'

The two men in black stood on either side of the kitchen door, their hands folded over their big stomachs. Jack felt nauseous. His hands shook.

'How much do they want?'

Had he said what he thought he said? *How much do they want?* Every phrase out of his mouth was one he would never have believed he would say.

Ramón grimaced. 'Ten K.'

'Ten what?'

'Ten K, ten large, ten g's. Ten thousand dollar, *guero*.'

He spoke sharply to his gang in Spanish. There was movement. Caballo reached into a black plastic bag, took out a Diet Coke and handed it to Ramón. It was beaded with condensation. Ramón opened it with a hiss and took a long drink. He belched. 'So?'

'So what?'

'So where we get the money? *Jack*.'

Jack glanced desperately at Carina. Her face was blank.

'Why are you asking me?'

'You think I have ten thousand dollar?'

'Well, I don't have it.'

'Of course not,' Ramón said. 'You are just country-club kid. But Howard … he have money.'

'My *dad*? How do you know my dad's name?'

Even as he spoke he remembered the moment from Friday night: *Well, Ramón, I am Howard Klements.*

'I can't tell my dad about this.'

Ramón leaned close. His breath smelled metallic. 'What, little Jack – you think this is school-yard shit? You think maybe is all a game? These crazies, they no get their money, what you think they do, huh?'

'I don't know.'

'I think maybe you have some idea. No?'

Jack said nothing. He just stared into Ramón's hard eyes.

'So, what you do?'

'I'll ask him. I guess.'

'*Muy bien.*'

Ramón nodded at the big guy who had searched Jack. He handed him Jack's wallet and keys. Ramón opened the wallet, found the eighty-five dollars Jack had put aside for his lunch date and removed it. 'Down payment,' he said, stuffing the bills in his pants pocket. 'Howard, he give the rest.' He gave Jack the empty wallet and keys. 'Carina meet you tomorrow. One o'clock. At the playfield.'

'Which one?' Jack said.

'Denny.'

'You really think my dad is going to give me ten thousand dollars tonight?'

'Hey. His decision. He come himself, that's cool. Or you tell Carina *que pasa* and we do it whatever way Howard want.' Ramón smiled. His teeth were dirty and crooked.

'Or not,' he said.

Behind him, Caballo smiled.

Outside the building, Jack stood on the walkway, trembling. Carina held his arm.

'My dad will go to the cops,' Jack said.

'No, he won't.'

'You don't know him.'

'I know you. You will explain.'

'Explain what? That my cousin's been kidnapped? This isn't the movies, Carina.'

'No. Is not.'

His empty wallet was still in his hand. He pocketed it. A police siren wobbled in the distance.

'He took my money. For our lunch.'

'For what?'

'Never mind.'

'I'm sorry,' she said.

'It's not your fault. But, I mean … you think he's going to bring that kind of money to Denny Playfield? My *dad*?'

'What about Feen?'

The way her hair had been pulled back in its pony-tail made her forehead and eyes bigger. Or was it the fear in her face? Yes, what about Finn? All this was about him, and yet it was as if he had nothing to do with it. But he had *caused* it.

'This is my cousin. My mom's nephew. How can my parents *not* go to the police?'

'Police would make worse. Feen would be hurt.'

She was crying. He touched her arm and she moved to him, hugging him tightly. A few days ago this embrace was everything he hoped for: the smell of her hair, the press of her face against his shoulder, the sound of her breathing in his ear.

But he felt no comfort. None at all.

16.

Going home on the camp bus, Jack remembered a TV show he had seen about a man on parole who was caught with stolen goods and sent back to prison. Handcuffed and dressed in an orange jump suit, he had been bussed through his neighbourhood on a sunny summer's day. The windows were covered by a metal grille, and through its mesh he could see the shops and parks and playgrounds where he had grown up. The man's face was without expression, but his point of view of the passing scene said it all. Behind bars, everything changes.

In some run-down drug dealer's hangout in West Seattle, Finn was sitting (tied up? handcuffed?) on a kitchen chair, rubbing the scar on his forearm and wondering what was going to happen. This was no video game. Jack rubbed his own scar. It tingled like a memory. What would he do in Finn's place? What could he do but wait to be saved?

He tried to concentrate. Everything depended on his next step. But the harder he focused, the more confused he grew. His palms were damp from panic. His brain was flying in ten different directions at once. The kids at the front of the bus sang. It was one of those ninety-nine-bottles-of-beer-on-the-wall songs that's supposed to pass the time but actually stretches it out. The sound of their voices scraped against his nerves. The wind whistled through the open windows. Heading north on Route 5, the cars flashed by, as blurred as a mirage.

When he was in the sixth grade, Jack and a couple of other kids sometimes gathered in the boys' bathroom and made each other pass out. One at a time, each would inhale deeply ten times and then hold his breath as another boy grasped him tight around the chest and lowered him gently to the tiled floor when he fainted. Waking, there was a moment of strangeness before full consciousness, when he didn't know where he was, and the sideways view of the tiled floor and the scuffed shoes of his friends was like part of a strange and disturbing dream. But real. Something is wrong, but what is it? And where am I?

That was how he felt now. Waking into something strange and awful. And real. He thought he had been scared before? He had never been. *This* was scared.

At the shopping mall he exited the bus and aimlessly wandered the line of stores, staring at the goods piled in the windows without really seeing them. He imagined what he might look like to passing shoppers: a bored kid with no friends and nothing in particular on his mind. When in fact a single question seethed in his head: what was he going to tell his parents?

A car beside him honked. Honked again. It was his mom. He had no choice but to get in.

'What are you doing over here?' she said.

'Nothing.'

'Your dad said you left your bikes at home this morning. Didn't you ask him to have me meet you off the bus?'

He'd forgotten.

'Where's Finn?' she said.

Her face seemed to him a cartoon face, stretched and bulging. 'Dad's home?' he said.

'He's working from home all week. He told you last night. What's the matter, Jack?'

They sat, engine running, behind a row of parked cars. She had turned on the hazard lights, and the steady clicking was like a nail being driven into Jack's head.

'Can you turn those off?' he said, pointing at the flashing button on the dashboard.

'Jack, I'm not meant to be parked here. I said, where's Finn? I don't have time for any messing.'

'I don't know.'

'Didn't he come home with you on the bus?'

'No.'

She frowned. Though she was perfectly still, her thumbs furiously rubbed the steering wheel. 'What did he tell you? Before you left camp.'

'He didn't tell me anything.'

'*What did he tell you?*'

'He's not coming back.'

'What are you talking about?'

She swivelled in her seat, looking through each window in turn, as if Finn had to be somewhere close by. In her agitation, she nudged the windshield-wiper stalk. The blades scraped and stuttered across the dry windscreen. She fumbled as she tried to turn them off and accidentally honked the horn. A man crossing in front of them stopped and stared, his jaw thrust forward.

Jack felt about to burst. 'He's *run away*,' he shouted.

***

The weird relief that Jack felt when he told this lie disappeared quickly. At the house he was pushed into a chair in the kitchen and grilled by his dad, who paced back and forth like a detective while Jack's mom huddled near the phone, her arms crossed and her shoulders hunched.

'That's all he said? *I'm not coming home.*'

'Don't shout, Howard.'

'Can I just get an answer to a simple question?'

'Tonight,' Jack said. 'He said he's not coming home *tonight.*'

'I have to ring Orla,' she said.

'You're not ringing anyone.'

'Don't speak to me like that.'

'Clare, I'm sorry. But can we just see where we are here first?' He leaned over Jack. His breath smelled of coffee. 'Does that mean he's coming home tomorrow?'

'Where will he go?' she said. Her voice was strained, as if she were about to cry. She had bags under her eyes. 'Tonight? Where will he sleep?'

'I don't know,' Jack said. 'I told you. *I don't know!*'

'Does this have anything to do with that gang?'

Jack didn't answer.

'What did I tell you,' his dad said, his arms flailing. 'You should never have let these kids go into the city. *Now* look.'

'You bring Jack in all the time.'

'What, to the club? To a ballgame? I'm *with* him. You let them go to a *lowrider* show. By themselves!'

'It doesn't have anything to do with the gang,' Jack said.

'How do you know?'

His mom had dropped her arms and stepped closer to

his dad. 'Maybe if you had been nicer to him. Spent a bit more time with him.'

'I haven't been here. I've been travelling.'

'Would you stop yelling at each other?' Jack said. 'He'll probably turn up at art camp tomorrow.'

Both his parents looked at him. Though her face looked stricken, his mom's voice grew hopeful.

'Do you really think so?'

His dad left the kitchen.

'Where are you going?' she said.

He shouted back, 'I have to make a phone call.'

'Howard!'

He went into his study. She crouched beside Jack and held his arm with both hands. She was trembling. 'Why would he do something like this?' she said. 'Has he no idea what this will do to his mother?'

'He's probably just hanging around all night.'

'With those gang boys?'

'No. Maybe with the art-school kids who live in the city.'

'Is that what he said?'

'Not really. But you know him. He just wants to be cool.'

As he had since his mom picked him up at the mall, Jack was making everything up as he went along. Buying time until he could meet Carina the next day. Though the whole situation seemed worse than hopeless. He had nothing he could tell his parents and nothing he could tell Ramón. And if his mom was this hysterical now, he couldn't imagine what she would be like if she knew the truth.

She moved across the kitchen, reached for the telephone, pulled back. 'Who's he ringing?' she said. 'My God, Jack, why did this have to happen? What am I going to say to Orla?'

He had a brainwave. It just came to him. He could arrange for one of Ramón's guys to steal his dad's Audi and give it to the other gang instead of the ransom. An Audi A5. Only a year old. That had to be worth a lot more than ten thousand, and his dad would get the insurance.

Thinking of this plan was like grabbing a life preserver. He could breathe again. He said, 'Mom, don't worry. Everything's going to be all right.'

She looked right through him.

His dad strode in, brisk and efficient. 'I called Lou Katchaturian.'

'Katchaturian?' she said. 'Like the composer?'

This comment irritated his dad, who raised his hand as if stopping traffic. 'He's head of security at my division. Ex-cop. He said we should call it in.'

'Call the police?'

'They used to make you wait twenty-four hours, but now they say make the report right away.'

'Oh, God.'

'Listen, Clare. The good news is his age. Lou said 99.9 per cent of kids over thirteen come back after one night. The stats are good.'

'*Stats?*' The call had calmed his dad, but Jack's mom

swayed like a tree in the wind, a low moaning sound coming from her throat.

'Who do we call?' she said, her voice cracking. 'The Bellevue police?'

'No. Seattle. You make the report in the place where he went missing.'

'Then what?'

'Lou gave me a freephone number. The Washington State Patrol have a unit. But we can't make that call until we've reported it to the local cops first. Where he went missing. We need to get them to enter him into a national database. Then we can call the MPU.'

'The what?'

'Missing Persons Unit.'

His mom sobbed like a woman at a funeral. Jack grew very uncomfortable. He hated to see his mother in this state, but what could he do? And what would she be like tomorrow? His dad put his arm around her and sent Jack to his room. Sitting on his bed, he listened to a long exchange of cries and whispers, followed by his dad on the phone again. It was getting dark, but he did not turn on the desk lamp. There had been no dinner and Jack discovered that he was hungry.

A Seattle police officer from the west precinct came to the house at nine o'clock. Before he arrived, Howard cooked some spaghetti while Clare lay down. They ate without conversation, exhausted by the tension. When the doorbell rang, Jack returned to his room. It had started raining. After another ten minutes of murmuring his dad summoned him to the kitchen.

The cop was a broad-faced man in plain clothes. He looked like a gym teacher and wore a beige shirt and a thin green tie underneath a baseball jacket mottled with wet patches. There was a shaving nick on his chin.

'How you doing, Jack? Take a seat there.' His wide smile made his face beefier. His nose was crooked but his eyes were kindly. 'My name is Steven. Here's what we're doing. I'm going to take some information from you and your parents about Finn and then ask you a few questions.'

'He'll probably just come back to the Institute tomorrow. By the end of the day.'

'That's good to hear. But let's just get this information down first so we can move to the next stage, OK? Think carefully before you answer. If you don't know, just tell me. No guesswork.'

First he asked for Finn's height, weight, and date of birth. Jack's mom brought out his passport, which recorded his birthday but not the other details.

'I don't think Irish passports have that information,' she said.

There was some argument about Finn's height. Was he taller than Jack or not? The discussion was very tense. Then Steven asked Jack to tell him the last time he saw Finn, whether he was acting strange, if there had been anyone unfamiliar hanging around the classrooms. Everything Jack said, even if it was vague or negative, the cop wrote in his notebook.

'What was he wearing?'

'Black T-shirt, black jeans,' his dad said.

'No,' Jack said. 'Not today. Today he wore blue jeans and a T-shirt with a skull on it. A red skull.'

Steven made a note.

'And a Dodgers cap,' Jack said. 'And a medallion and chain. Silver.'

'Shoes?'

'Black Converse.'

Steven nodded approvingly.

'Any distinguishing features? Birthmarks, moles, so forth.'

'He has a lot of acne,' his dad said.

'Anything else?'

'No,' Jack said.

His dad said, 'What about the scar on his arm?'

'What kind of scar?'

'It's nothing,' Jack said. 'He cut himself in school.'

'It's some sort of symbol,' his dad said.

'A gang symbol,' his mom said.

Steven turned to Jack.

'I guess. Yeah.'

'Like a tattoo?' Steven said.

After a few moments of silence, his dad said, 'He carved it into his arm. Himself.'

Steven slid the pad and pen across the table. He said to Jack, 'Could you draw it for me?'

Pen hovering above the paper, Jack hesitated. Steven watched him, his hands folded on the tabletop. Jack made a few strokes with the pen and slid the drawing back to Steven. His face tightened. It was a tiny change, but the whole feeling of the room altered.

'This guy Ramón,' Steven said.

'What guy?'

'*Jack*,' his dad said, his voice very tight.

Steven raised his arm, calming him. 'The gang member you and your parents met on the Fourth of July. The gentleman who seemed to know you and Finn.'

Jack told the cop the same story he had told his parents.

'And you haven't seen him since? Think carefully, Jack. At the camp. On the bus. In one of the parks maybe. You haven't seen him since the lowrider show?'

'Well, on the Fourth.'

'Apart from that.'

The three adults stared at him intensely. The overhead light made his eyes smart. The trouble he was in now would be no worse if he lied. He focused on his dad's car. Imagined the keys sitting in the ceramic bowl in his study. If he could get a copy made. Or find the spare. There must be a spare.

'No,' he said. 'I haven't seen him since. And I don't think Finn has either.'

17.

Jack's parents did not go to bed until very late, and he woke several times to the sound of their voices and the patter of rain on the window. In between, he had vague, scattered dreams he couldn't remember but which made him feel depressed. Above, the wooden slats of the upper bunk glowed in the half-light like prison bars, and the mattress, for the first time in weeks, did not bulge through.

Much of his time awake he spent planning how to get into the city by one o'clock. His dad hadn't said he *shouldn't* go to camp, but what if he told Jack in the morning that he had to stay home? How would he meet Carina? He thought about it and figured that the best strategy would be to do his route and head off to the bus as usual. Maybe his parents wouldn't even be up. But if they were and they said anything, he would argue that the other students might know where Finn was. Or that he could check the places where they went to lunch.

He rose at four. The newspapers were on the front step, covered in plastic to protect against the damp. The route took forever, not only because he'd got used to Finn doing half, but also because he was worried about looking for the spare key to the Audi when he got home. His dad didn't get up until six, and maybe after the late night he'd sleep another hour.

When Jack returned to the house it was a quarter after five. It was still dark, and the rain drummed against the roof. He hung his dripping jacket and paper satchel on their hooks and left his wet shoes on the deck. The cat meowed and he let her outside. He crept down the hallway and put his ear to his parents' bedroom door. Nothing. The study was across the hall. Feeling like a criminal, he turned the handle and slipped inside, leaving the door ajar. His dad had a couple of computers in the room that he always left on. They hummed and blinked in the morning gloom.

He tried searching for the key in the dark, but it was no use. He turned on the desk lamp. The click was like a clap of thunder. Slowly, carefully, he opened each drawer. His dad wasn't exactly tidy. Each drawer had its distinct mess and the search took a long time. Every few minutes he cocked an ear, but his parents' room stayed silent. After the desk, there was the filing cabinet, some accordion files, two boxes, and four beer steins that his dad had bought in Germany, perched on the top shelf of the bookcase and overflowing with bric-à-brac and whatever he emptied from his pockets.

The key was in the second stein. Finding it was like Christmas morning.

The door creaked.

'What are you doing in here?'

His dad stood in the doorway, rumpled and severe. Jack had pocketed the key and could feel its silver shape against the side of his leg. What had he seen?

'Oh, hi Dad.'

'Are you going through my things?'

'I'm looking for my collection book.'

'And you think it's in *here*?'

'Mom said she put it away. I thought it … you know. And I have to collect tonight.'

His dad surveyed the room, scratching his stomach. 'Everything that's going on around here and you're thinking about collecting?'

Jack shrugged. 'I don't have Finn to help me.'

'Sheesh. Don't let your mother hear you say that.'

In the kitchen his dad poured two bowls of cereal. Sleepiness had softened his usual rough edges. Jack took milk from the fridge. They ate in silence, looking through the rain-streaked window at the slowly brightening sky.

'You should go to camp,' his dad said.

'You think so?'

'Lou said so. Chances are, Finn will be there. If he doesn't show up I don't know what's going to happen with your mom. She's all over the place as it is.'

'He probably won't turn up until the afternoon.'

At this comment his dad frowned but didn't say anything. He took a bite of cereal and spoke with his mouth full. 'I'll give you Mom's cell phone. If he's there when you arrive, you call me. If he's not, text me a half hour after you arrive.'

'Text and say what?'

'That he's not there. Then send me an update every half hour. And don't say anything to the teachers. If the principal calls, I'll deal with it.'

'You don't want me to tell the teachers?'

'No.'

Jack couldn't imagine any of his friends' parents saying this. His dad sure liked to be in control.

'How about if you don't hear from me,' Jack said, 'it means he hasn't turned up.'

'Just send the texts.' He unplugged the phone from the charger. 'Here. I'll show you how to do it.'

'*Dad*. I know how to send a text.'

The bus was late and the driver was in a bad mood. Something was wrong with the engine. The rain had thickened and the inside of the bus smelled like damp fabric and burning motor oil. The other kids were pleased with the delay and while the driver poked under the hood they ran up and down the aisle, shouting and hitting each other over the head with rolled-up newspapers. Jack pleaded silently for the bus to start. The morning traffic slid past, brake-lights and indicators dripping red and yellow through the blurred windows. When one of the kids hit him, Jack grabbed the paper baton and threw it on the floor. The kid pointed at him and bleated, 'Loser!'

They got going at last. 'You're all going to be late,' the driver yelled as he climbed into his seat, 'and there ain't a damn thing I can do about it.' The sky was dark with low cloud, and the cars on the highway had their lights on. Halfway over the floating bridge the bus broke down. Steam or smoke billowed from the engine. The kids cheered; the driver cursed. Red-faced and breathless, he dialled a number on his mobile phone and waved his free arm in a way that was supposed to be threatening but just looked funny. After receiving instructions, he herded everyone to the back of the bus, close to the emergency exit, in case a fire broke out.

'Now stay put,' he said, ''less I tell you otherwise. Dangerous situation here.'

The state patrol arrived within minutes, then a mechanic, twenty minutes later. Jack sent a text to his dad. The phone rang within thirty seconds. His mom's ringtone was a song from *The Lion King*, which made the other kids laugh. Jack hit the red button. It rang again.

'What do you mean you're stuck on the highway?' his dad said. His voice was loud enough to be heard by everyone.

'The bus broke down.'

Jack tried to edge away from the others, but they were all crammed together at the back.

'Call me as soon as you get there.'

'Yes, Dad,' one of the kids said.

More laughter. Jack's stomach blazed with nervousness.

It was nearly ten o'clock by the time they got to the Institute. Jack joined his life-drawing class, which was nearly finished. The teacher asked about Finn. She had assumed he was on the bus with the rest of the delayed kids. Jack explained that they were cousins and Finn had stayed with other relatives in the city last night and had said to Jack he might be coming along to camp, but it wasn't surprising that he had not shown up because they were going to Mount Rainier for the day. She said he would have to tell the principal.

Through the rest of the morning, Jack sent texts to his

dad as planned and rehearsed what he would say to
Ramón. At twelve-thirty he left the building. The rain had
stopped. His mouth was dry and his legs shaky. As he
walked along Vine Street he had the odd sensation that
what was happening was both present and past. *He walked
down Vine. He reached the playfield.* As if he were a character
in a story.

He was early. He waited for Carina beside the
basketball court, watching the pick-up game without
taking it in and fingering the car key in his pocket. He
could not help picturing Finn in terrifying imprisonment,
waiting for salvation. And Jack – Jack who wasn't even in
high school yet – was going to be his saviour? The
prospect was distant and unreal, but it was all he could do
not to throw up.

He didn't see her coming. He was sending a text to his
dad when she tapped him on the shoulder. He jumped
and she laughed nervously.

'It's me,' she said. 'Only me.' Her assurances did not
get rid of the tension. Her face was pale and puffy, like
yesterday, and her hair tangled. She continued smiling, as
if happy to see him, but something was different beneath
her skin.

A basketball banged against the mesh beside them,
making him jump again.

'Let's go over there,' she said.

They walked across the field to the grove of trees. Her
usual smoothness had altered: her gait was jerky with extra
movement, like a puppet on a kids' TV show. She wore

slashed jeans and a white T-shirt and sneakers that had traces of red mud along the edges of the heels. The relaxed girl with silver jewellery and an easy smile had been replaced by someone completely different, tense and wary and dishevelled. But still lovely. The gang kids had disappeared from the grove, though a few couples leaned against the tree trunks, embracing and kissing, unaware of anything but their passion. As he and Carina had clutched each other in the alley doorway. Was that really less than a week ago?

'Just so you know,' he said, 'I don't have the money.'

She seemed to think about this, then said, 'Police?'

'No. No police.'

She nodded. 'Is OK you no have the money.'

'OK? How is it OK?'

She looked over her shoulder, as if someone might be listening. 'Last night, I hear Ramón and Arturo in the kitchen. They don't know I can hear.'

'Who is Arturo?'

'The one they call Panza. With the big belly and the beard. He say to Ramón that Feen is no eating his food.'

'The other gang is telling him this?'

'No other gang. *They* have Feen.'

'Ramón?'

'Yes.'

'You're sure?'

'*Absolutamente.*'

'But they *like* him.'

She grimaced. 'They like money, is what they like.'

So they had been lying. Why should that surprise him? These boys were criminals. And it was possible that Carina was lying now. Her words could be another step in their plan. *If he doesn't come with the money, tell him we have Feen.*

But the way she tilted her head, her lower lip trembling, her eyes sad, made him certain that she was telling the truth. She was turning against her tribe to help two boys from another world. Putting herself at risk. Jack wanted to hug her, to tell her everything was all right, even though he was the one with the problem. But he couldn't, maybe because he was remembering all the lies *he* had told: to his parents, to the cop, to Carina herself. No police, he had said, concealing the truth without hesitation. Should he come clean?

'So, what do we do?' he said.

She straightened her shoulders and her face filled with a certainty of its own. 'Come with me.'

'Why? Where are we going?'

'Just come.'

18.

They were keeping Finn, she told him, in the same house in High Point. She had seen Arturo carrying a bag of food to one of the back rooms, and when she asked Ramón about it he had laughed and said that Panza had a big appetite.

'Why are they hiding this from you?'

'I'm just a *chica*,' she said, curling her upper lip. 'That's what they think. Just a little girl.'

'At least they're giving him food.'

They were sitting at the back of the number 21 bus. The rain had stopped and the sun was out and the surface of the street was steaming like a battlefield. The side of her thigh pressed against his, and as she spoke her hands moved through the air like small birds.

'But he is no eating. That's what Arturo said.'

'He's scared.'

'I don't know.'

He reached across and held her hand.

'It's going to be all right,' he said. 'I have the whole thing worked out.'

He slid the key from his pocket and showed it to her. He told her about his idea of letting one of Ramón's guys steal the Audi.

'He comes late at night, drives it away. Nobody will ever know. And my dad gets the insurance money.'

She withdrew her hand from his. 'Are you crazy?'

'It's so simple. And the car, it's worth more than ten thousand.'

Her eyes grew wide. 'Of course is worth more. Is worth *fifty* thousand. Why you give them more than what they ask? Five times. And, watch this, they know where you live. You think they stop with car?'

'What else would they want?'

'They want everything you have. What you and your family have. You are rich and Ramón, he is poor. Like Robin Hood, but with guns.'

'I've never seen any guns.'

She smiled a weary, grown-up smile. 'You think that because you no see something, is not there?'

It was as if she had rejected him along with his plan. Fear jumbled in his chest with confusion and attraction. He had thought that this shared ordeal was bringing them together, but she was slowly slipping away.

'So why are we going there,' he said, 'if it's so dangerous?'

The phone rang. His dad's number appeared on the screen. He stared at the blinking number but knew that if he didn't answer, he would keep calling and calling. There was no escaping his parents.

'Hi, Dad.'

'You didn't text.' His voice was loud and edgy.

'Sorry. I was out of range.'

'Where are you? Your mother is worried sick. Is that traffic?'

'I'm walking down to the park where we usually eat lunch. In case he's there.'

'Why would he be there?'

'I don't know. He might be.'

'Are you by yourself?'

'Of course I am.'

'You didn't say anything to the teachers, did you?'

'I made an excuse.'

'Check quick and go straight back to the Institute. You hear me?'

After hanging up Jack turned off the phone. His hands shook.

'That was your father?'

'Yeah.'

'He no know.'

'Of course not.'

They got off the bus two stops away from the house, in front of a corner store with a wire rack of Spanish-language newspapers and neat baskets of passion-fruit and rice, white beans and sweet potatoes lined up beneath a striped awning. Carina went into the shop and spoke briefly to a middle-aged woman behind the counter. The woman nodded and Carina motioned Jack inside. At the rear they went through a low door into a dark kitchen area with a hot plate and a Formica-topped table. The room smelled strongly of spices and overripe fruit.

She closed the door and they sat at the table.

'I have a plan,' Carina said in a low voice that blended into the darkness and smells and rising tension. 'The room with Feen is at back of the house. We go up the alley and I show you the window.'

'What if they see us?'

'All the windows have board on them. They no see.'

His eyes were growing used to the dark. Above the hot plate was a Puerto Rican flag. Beside it was a tapestry of the Virgin Mary, who wore a long green robe embroidered with gold stars and stood on a broad crescent held by the outstretched arms of a baby-faced angel.

Carina got up from her chair and took something from the cupboard beneath the hot plate. It was a crowbar. She laid it on the table between them. It was ugly and battered, and whatever sense of adventure had remained now turned to fear. 'You wait in alley. With this. After ten minutes you use to take board off the window and Feen come out.'

He was relieved to hear he was not going to have to hit someone with it.

'What about you?' he said.

'I get Ramón out of the house. And others. All except Arturo. Arturo will stay, so you must be quick with board.'

'Is he in the room with Finn?'

'No. In other room. You must be quick.'

'How will you get them out? The others?'

She rose from the chair and bowed before the tapestry and made the sign of the cross. She prayed silently for a few moments. 'Our Lady of Guadalupe will guide me,' she said. 'Once you pray to the Virgin, she no fail you.'

He stood up and lifted the crowbar. It was heavy.

'Carina.'

She put up both hands. 'We must go. Now.'

Her face had the artificial glow of an icon and her eyes

would not meet his. It was obvious by now: the more she helped him, the more distance stretched between them.

In the alley they crouched behind some garbage cans and Carina pointed out the plywood-covered window of Finn's prison. The kitchen where they had been the day before, with its open windows, was around the side, and she warned him not to wander into its sightlines.

'Ten minutes,' she said.

He checked his watch. It was nearly two o'clock. His dad would be going nuts wondering why he hadn't sent a text or answered his calls.

'Then you go to the window. Exactly ten. When you are out, with Feen, go that way.' She nodded up the alley-way, opposite the way they had come. 'You have money?'

'A little.'

'You get a taxi. Where the alley cross the road.'

She laid a hand on his arm for a second and moved away.

'Carina.'

She stopped but stared at the ground.

'What will you tell them?' he said. 'To get them out of the house?'

She shook her head. 'Don't worry.'

'And when will I see you again?'

She shrugged and looked at the boarded-up house, with its peeling paint, rust stains along the roof, graffiti lacing the doors and plywood. 'Just get Feen out, OK?'

'OK.'

She crept away. He watched her as she turned the corner and disappeared from view. She didn't look back.

He waited. The seconds dripped by. The minutes were like hours. The sound of children shouting nearby disturbed him. What if he was seen? A kid hiding behind a garbage can with a crowbar in his hand. In Bellevue the cops would have picked him up by now.

Four minutes. Six minutes. Eight. His stomach churned. His teeth chattered. He felt the urge to go to the toilet.

Coming up to the ten-minute mark, a door beside the boarded window opened. A door Jack hadn't even noticed was there. Finn came out. He scurried down the steps, peered up and down the alleyway, then faced the back wall of the house, legs spread. Slowly, Jack rose and edged towards him, keeping an eye on the open door, expecting to see Arturo poke his head out at any moment.

Finn was pissing against the base of the wall. As he finished, he turned, zipping up his jeans, and jerked back when he saw Jack.

'Jaysus, what are you doing here? Scared the shite out of me.'

The medallion and hat were missing, but he still wore the death's head shirt, food-stained down the front.

'How did you get out?' Jack whispered.

'There's no toilet inside. Bursting so I was.'

'Did she get them all to leave? Where is Arturo?'

Finn frowned. He seemed confused.

'C'mon,' Jack said. 'Let's go. She told me to go this way. We can get a taxi.'

But Finn didn't move.

'We're here to save you, Finn. Carina and me.'

'Save me from what?'

'Have they hypnotised you or something? Don't you know what's going on? Ramón wants my dad to pay to let you go. Ten thousand dollars.'

Still Finn offered nothing but a calm, cold stare.

'*C'mon*,' Jack said.

'Why?'

'You're in danger. They have guns.'

'Guns?' Finn laughed. 'Oh yeah. Like they're going to shoot *me*.'

Something clicked for Jack, like when he was in math class and some small, obvious detail made a whole theorem become clear.

'You're in on it, aren't you?'

Finn pushed his bottom lip out and said nothing.

'You're helping them to steal from my dad. From your uncle.'

'It's not stealing.'

Jack hit him on the shoulder with the crowbar. Not full strength, but hard enough to hurt.

Finn staggered back. 'You fucking madman,' he yelled, 'what are you doing?'

'*I'm* a madman? The cops were at our house yesterday. They're out there right now looking for you. You're in a national database as a missing person. My mom was crying all night.'

As he shouted, Jack grew more frenzied. He was afraid he was going to hit Finn full force, so he threw the crowbar hard against the side of the house and it bounced off and clattered to the ground.

You're ruining my life, he wanted to say, but his throat was clogged with rage. Tears coursed along the wings of his nose. He had imagined Finn tied to a chair, scared for his life, but it was Jack who had been bound down. All the tension of the last two days flowed out of him, leaving a huge hollowness in his chest and a desperate certainty that he would never see Carina again.

'Calm down,' Finn said, his voice guilty. 'It's no big deal.'

Jack walked away, sobbing and wiping his eyes.

'Where are you going?' Finn shouted.

Jack waved the words away.

'I'm staying here,' Finn said, less sure this time.

Jack kept walking. Soon he heard the shuffle of feet and Finn fell in step beside him. As they reached the road, Finn said, 'It was all a piss-take, you know. They were never going to take any money off you.'

Jack sniffled and said nothing.

'Did they really call the cops?'

19.

By the time Jack's parents picked them up outside the Institute, Finn had a story worked out. The day before, he and Jack had had an argument, a silly fight about a lost hat. Finn refused to join Jack on the bus, and as Jack climbed aboard, Finn shouted through the open window that he was running away. Jack was mad, so he hadn't said anything to the driver.

After the bus left, Finn had wandered up to the Seattle Centre, where he met three Irish guys drinking in the park behind the Key Arena. They were decent, he said, homeless lads who had come to the city twenty years ago looking for work in the building trade but couldn't get jobs because they weren't legal. He felt sorry for them and thought he'd keep them company for a few hours. One of them had a desperate cough. They wanted to hear about Dublin, had him scrounge cigarettes for them, sang ballads until they were hoarse. The next thing he knew it was after midnight and he had no choice but to stay with them. He'd no money to make a phone call and figured it would be safer to wait until morning and meet Jack at the Institute.

Sitting in the back seat of the car, allowing Finn to describe this imaginary escapade to his parents, Jack was numb and hopeless. He hated going along with Finn's lies, but what else could he do? Tell them what had really happened? Kidnap, ransom, double-cross, carjacking, guns, threats – words from a TV screen, not from life. They would have laughed at him. Or thought he was crazy. Suddenly, the truth was distant and unreal. It was as if the whole episode had been a video game.

And the way Finn told the story, it sounded as if he believed it himself. Jack's mom bought it, that was for sure.

'Why didn't you tell us about the fight?' she said to Jack. She could not be serious. Even this she blamed on him.

'The whole thing was stupid.'

'You told us he ran away.'

'He did run away.'

'But after the two of you'd had an argument. If we'd known the truth, it would have been less frightening. We would have understood. A little, at least.'

'I didn't tell him not to come home.'

'Jack, he's your *cousin*.'

'It was my fault,' Finn said. 'Not Jack's.'

'Were you drinking?' Jack's dad asked. His voice was hard.

'No.'

'You spent all night with a couple of winos and you didn't have a drink?'

'No, I didn't.'

'And you decided to go back to the Institute in the morning. Right?'

'Yeah.'

'So how come you didn't show up until after lunch?'

'Just, you know, by the time I got there.'

'By the time you got there.'

'Yeah.'

Jack saw his dad's eyes reflected in the rear-view mirror. They were shiny with anger.

The police were not surprised to hear that Finn had shown up unharmed. Teenagers went missing for a night or two all the time – the stats were the stats – and once Finn was home and Jack's dad had called the Seattle police, the case was closed. But because his name had been entered into the MPU database, a counsellor had to come to the house and interview Finn the next day. The meeting happened in the study, privately, and when Finn came out he smirked at Jack while the counsellor, a heavy woman in dungarees with braided grey hair, spoke loudly to Jack's parents, saying that Finn was an impressive young man with 'empathy for the disadvantaged' and 'an inner strength unusual for his age'.

Jack's mom smiled with relief, but his dad was not convinced. And after he saw the social worker to her car, he sent Jack to his room and sat Finn down at the kitchen table. Jack listened from his bedroom door.

'What did your mother say last night?'

When Jack's dad couldn't reach him on the phone, Clare had panicked and called her sister. So the first thing Finn had to do when they got home was call Orla.

'Nothing, really.'

'Do you have any idea of the suffering you caused her? Not to mention your aunt.'

'She goes mental over the tiniest thing.'

'*The tiniest thing?*'

Jack's mom came into the kitchen; he heard her heels on the tiled floor.

'She was so *concerned*, Finn,' she said. 'And she had a right to know.'

'Why did you have to tell her, anyway?' Finn said.

'Why did she tell your mother,' his dad said very slowly, 'that her son, who we have the responsibility of caring for, had *not come home*?' He was getting really mad and Finn didn't seem to be aware of it.

'What did she say to you about it?' she said. 'About what happened?'

'Nothing.'

'She wants you to go back to Ireland,' his dad said.

'No she doesn't.'

'What do you want, Finn?' she said.

'To stay here.'

The legs of his dad's chair scraped the tiles. His voice came from a different part of the room. And it was louder. 'It doesn't matter what he wants,' he said. 'He scared the heck out of us and his mother. He's lost our trust.'

'Howard!'

'Whatever Orla says, we do. That's final.'

'You know Orla. She'll calm down in a day or two.'

But it was Howard who didn't calm down. He and Clare had a long conversation in the study that night. At breakfast the next morning he announced that he had changed Finn's return flight to Dublin from late August to this coming Sunday. He had two days left in Seattle. Jack's dad was travelling to California on business on Monday morning, and though he didn't say so, Jack knew he wanted Finn gone before he left. Finn turned pale at the news.

The boys had not spoken to each other since arriving home. For two nights they had slept in the same room without even a glance passing between them. All day Thursday, as Finn slyly celebrated how easily he had fooled Jack's mom, and Jack bristled over his betrayal, they had hung around the house and back yard, forbidden to leave the property, avoiding each other as best they could. So for Jack, his dad's decision was sweet. *Yes, send him back. That will wipe the smile off his face.*

But the tension only increased. And the boredom. The TV was off limits. The computer had been removed from the kitchen. After breakfast, Howard drove to work, but Clare stayed home from her gardening club and made the boys weed the flower patch and trim the hedges and spread compost. They worked, against their will, shoulder to shoulder. Finn listened to his iPod. The day was hot and still, and from the back yard Jack could hear the sound of motor boats and the laughter of swimmers.

In the afternoon, Finn disappeared into the bedroom. His mom allowed Jack to invite Jimmy Choi over to play badminton, and they set up the net beside the deck. They played several games and drank lemonade and Jimmy talked about school. He was on the chess team and in the science club and had been taking advanced math at Bellevue during the summer. He explained how he wanted to study astrophysics at Cal Tech. He might as well have been speaking Korean. It wasn't that Jack didn't understand what he said, but the detail had no meaning. Was Jack really going to high school in September? Last year he couldn't wait to be in Bellevue. But the hollowness he'd felt behind the house in High Point on Wednesday had stayed with him. He didn't care about anything anymore. Except seeing Finn leave.

His mom appeared at the door with Finn. She had a hand on his shoulder.

'Finn wants to play as well.'

'No, I don't.'

'Go on. You need the fresh air.'

She practically pushed him onto the deck. But Finn wouldn't play and Jack wouldn't talk to him and Jimmy didn't know what was going on. He just looked from one to the other.

'By the way, how come you guys aren't at art camp?'

Neither answered.

'How about round robin? You guys can start.'

But the air had turned sour. Finn carefully inserted the earbuds of his iPod and Jimmy shrugged and went home. Jack aimlessly bounced the shuttlecock on his racket while Finn sat on the edge of the deck and picked at the scar on his arm until it bled. Clare watched them through the kitchen window, wiping her hands on her apron.

They were sent to bed early. The night stayed hot, and Jack tossed in his bunk, unable to sleep, sweating and trying to ignore the heat and the crickets and the tumble of questions in his mind. Whenever the mattress bulged as Finn shifted above him, Jack seethed with anger.

After a while, he got out of bed and turned on the desk lamp and leafed through a sports magazine. Finn lay in bed with his face to the wall.

The magazine quivered. It took a moment for Jack to realise that his hands were shaking.

He couldn't be silent any longer. 'Did Carina know?' he said.

Finn didn't answer.

'I know you're awake.'

Jack went to the bed and shook Finn's shoulder.

'Leave me alone.'

'Did she know?'

'Know what?'

'About your stupid plan.'

No response. Jack shook him again. He turned suddenly. His eyes were red-rimmed and puffy. 'Is that all you care about?' Finn said. 'They're making me go back, and all you can think about is her?'

A week ago Jack would have felt sorry for him. But not tonight. There was so much that Finn should have to pay for. 'It's your own fault you're going back. If they knew what really happened it would be a lot worse.'

'How could it be worse? You have no idea how shite my life is back there. How miserable I'll be.'

'Then why did you make *me* so miserable?'

Finn flopped back on the mattress. 'Jays', it was only a bit of craic. We were only messin'.'

'Don't you care about me? Or Carina? What if she's in trouble?'

'She's not in trouble.'

'Why – because was she in on the whole thing?'

Finn laughed. 'Don't worry. Your precious little Carina didn't know a thing. It was all about fooling the two of youse.'

'So she put herself in danger to help you, and the whole time you were pretending. That's so *sick*.'

'What's sick is how thick you are. You haven't a clue.'

'Ramón will know. She got them to leave the house, and he'll figure it out and they'll hurt her.'

'What have you got against Ramón?'

'He's a criminal.'

'You don't know him. You hate him and the others just like your parents do. And for the same reason.'

'Why's that?'

'Because they're not like you.'

'They robbed me, Finn. And they blackmailed me. *You* blackmailed me.' He grabbed Finn's arm. 'How do I know they're not going to hurt her?'

'Because,' Finn shouted, 'she's *one of them*.'

Finn shoved him away and turned his face to the wall. Jack stepped back and watched his cousin's shoulders rise and fall as he breathed. Sweat dripped from Jack's forehead into his eyes. His hands had not stopped shaking.

The crickets blared. He wiped his face and went to the open window and looked at the world outside as if at a picture: winking stars, moonlight streaming through cottonwood leaves, the curve of the street lost in shadow. Somewhere in the distance a radio was tuned to a ball game. A screen door slammed.

Nothing out there was clear. Here, inside – in this room, this house, this family – he knew where he stood.

He rubbed the scar on his wrist. Finn sniffled and shifted in the bed, nursing his wounded feelings. *They're not like you*. Same as his cousin, Jack was different. What had made him think otherwise?

20.

Finn left on Sunday. After the endless hours of Saturday, hot and housebound, his exit happened quickly. He packed after an early breakfast. Jack's mom had bought him a new suitcase and given him gifts for Orla and his sisters: a coffee tumbler and a picture book, ballet slippers and two Abercrombie and Fitch tops. Howard put the suitcase in the trunk of the car. He was not going to the airport.

He shook Finn's hand. 'No hard feelings, huh?'

'Thanks for everything,' Finn mumbled and ducked into the back seat. Jack's dad couldn't get back into the house quick enough.

Jack wanted to stay at home, but his mom made him go. He sat in the front. Finn's iPod buzzed so loudly that Jack could make out the lyrics above the sounds of the car's air conditioning.

> *You ain't got enough bullets to see me bleed*
> *You fire up the crowd then three miss me*
> *You wanna diss my* varrio, *homie think again*

They cruised along Route 405 in the sunshine. His mom kept glancing at the mirror. Jack could tell she wanted to talk, but Finn wouldn't have heard her. He was slumped in the seat, lost to the music, eyes shut. He wore the same clothes he'd arrived in a month ago, right down to the knit cap and Xbox T-shirt.

She turned on the radio. Bluegrass competed with the thud of the rap. Jack watched the landscape peel past: Lake Washington to his right, Mount Rainier ahead in the glittering distance. It was the same drive they'd made when they picked him up, but in reverse. Like a tape rewinding.

A month, was that all? On Saturday afternoon, while his mom shopped and his dad worked and Finn sulked in the bedroom, Jack had called Carina's old number. As the phone rang his heart did its own gangsta beat and his throat went dry.

A male voice answered. 'Yo.'

'Ah, is Carina there?'

'*Quién?*'

'Carina?'

The guy hung up. Jack had run onto the deck and taken several deep breaths.

Clare parked beside the international terminal and they walked across the skyway and into the high, bright space with the P-51 suspended from the ceiling. They took the escalator to the departure desks. Finn still had the iPod blaring. As they waited in line, Clare busied herself with the paperwork while the boys stared in opposite directions. Holidaymakers in flowered shirts and straw hats surrounded them. They were flying out to Hawaii and spoke and laughed too loudly. The swirl and echo of their voices mixed with the bland terminal music and the tinny ball of sound floating around Finn. Jack's head hurt.

Approaching the security gate, his mom chattered nervously, sounding more and more Irish as she went on: 'Now tell your mother I was asking for her and she's welcome here any time, as well as the girls, of course, and yourself. I put the sweets in your carry-on. Keep your money safe and get some lunch in Chicago. Remember, you don't have to change terminals, and you have boarding passes for all the flights, and don't lose your passport, and you know we were delighted to have you and … oh, *Finn.*'

Tearful, she clutched him tightly, and his face appeared above her shoulder, as pale and spotted as the moon. She let go of him, patting him on the cheek as if he were five years old. She was crying full on now. He spent more time than he needed checking his carry-on bag and passport and boarding pass.

Finally he nodded at Jack. 'See ya.'

'Yeah. See ya.'

He swivelled as if to head to the security line then suddenly lurched back and hugged Jack. 'I'm sorry,' he whispered into his ear. Then he kissed Jack's mom and moved off, waving without looking back, his T-shirt untucked, the seat of his pants drooping.

Jack and his mom were silent all the way home. When they pulled into the driveway and his mom turned off the car, neither moved to get out. Both stared straight ahead, listening to the random tick of the cooling engine and the swish of the wind in the trees. The hood of the car flickered with the shifting shadows of leaves.

'It's a long way home for him,' she said.

'Yeah.'

'Do you think he'll be all right?'

'Do you mean on the trip or when he gets back?'

Her face crumpled and she shook her head and got out of the car.

In the month that followed, Jack was busy. He had fallen behind on his collecting, and with a lot of his customers coming and going on vacation he spent many evenings retracing his paper route, knocking on doors. During the day he mowed lawns and did some weeding and spade-work for women in his mom's gardening club. He got his book list from the high school and bought school supplies at Lakeshore Learning Store. His dad entered him in a tennis tournament at Killarney Glen Park, but Danny Smoltz beat him in the first round.

'Whatever happened to that Irish kid?' Danny asked. 'With the hat?'

They were drinking Gatorade after the game, beside a fold-up table behind the tennis courts. Jimmy's whole gang was there.

'He went back to Ireland.'

'I heard he got, like, deported,' Zach Lopach said.

Jimmy walked over to the table to refill his cup.

'They don't deport kids, you moron,' Danny said.

'Why not? What if he planted a bomb or something?'

'My cousin did not plant a bomb.'

'I didn't say he did. I said *what if.*'

Brandon Eberhardt said, 'I heard Megan Connors got this tattoo on her back. Of a butterfly.'

'It's not real,' Danny said. 'It's one of those ones that wears away.'

Zach spat a green stream of Gatorade onto the ground between his feet. 'She is such a slut.'

After the tournament, Jack steered clear of Jimmy's friends. He talked a lot on the phone with Cody and Jason from his grade-school class. Like him, they were excited about starting at Bellevue High. They lived in Newcastle, which was a short bike ride away, but he wasn't allowed to visit them. His dad hadn't exactly grounded him, but he was strict about where Jack could go. In early August, Cody invited him to the music festival on Alki Beach, but his dad said no. A flat no without any discussion. So Jack hung around the house and worked in the neighbourhood and watched the Mariners, who had lost Ichiro Suzuki to injury and were playing terribly.

The day after he told Jack he couldn't go to the concert, Howard called him into his study. A new laptop sat on his desk, open and running, beside his own.

'What do you think?' his dad said.

'That's mine?'

'Told you you'd get one for high school.'

Jack reached for the touchpad but his dad stayed his hand. 'Not yet. I'm putting Windows 7 on for you, and Office. Plus, there are some manuals you should look at before you get going. And I'm installing some filtering software.'

'What's that?'

'It will protect you from inappropriate sites on the web.'

'*Dad.*'

He folded the laptop shut. 'Don't look so disappointed.'

'I'm not. It's great. Thanks.'

His dad cleared his throat. 'You know what this is, don't you? I mean as well as being a laptop.'

'Uh … no.'

'It's a symbol. It represents responsibility. Do you know what that means?'

He was like Mrs. Lawson at Bellevue High, pointing at the signs with the big words.

'I have to look after it?'

'Well, you do, of course, but what I mean is, you're moving to a new stage in your life, one where you have more freedom. It's up to you to take responsibility for your actions. To be accountable.'

'OK.'

'Everything that happened this summer, let's put that behind us, right? You made some bad decisions, but now it's time to mature. To start acting like an adult instead of like a kid.'

He stared at him. Jack didn't know what he was supposed to say.

'The desktop,' his dad said, 'that we had in the kitchen?'

'Yeah?'

'My guy in work did an audit on it.' He raised his eyebrows in that way he did. *You know what I found there. You tell me what it means.*

'Finn went on it a lot,' Jack said. 'Early in the morning, after the route. Mom said he could once, but I think he sort of took advantage.'

'You see, this is the kind of thing I mean.'

'What kind of thing?'

But his dad's attention had drifted. His fingers drummed the surface of the laptop.

'Your mom thinks I was too hard on Finn. What do you think?'

Jack shrugged.

'You don't have an opinion?'

'No,' Jack said, 'you weren't too hard on him.'

He kept talking as if Jack hadn't agreed with him. 'I don't think you appreciate how foolish and dangerous his behaviour was. I'm not just talking about the grief he gave your mom and Orla. I mean about himself. What could have happened to him. Staying out all night like that, associating with these homeless guys. Don't get me wrong; they're victims, I know that, but alcohol and drug use and mental problems have put them in a very violent world. Finn could have been hurt. It's amazing he wasn't. What is it about you kids? You act like this sort of stuff is nothing.'

'No, we don't.'

'You could have stepped up. Individually. Let me know what was going on and played your part. Been *mature*. Instead, you behave like you'll never get hurt. Like life is one big video game.'

'I don't play video games. You won't let me.'

His dad turned to his own laptop. 'That's enough for now.'

Jack had an urge to defend himself, but what could he say? He got up to leave. As he was closing the study door, his dad said, 'I just did what I thought was right for the family.'

'I know.'

'Do you? Well, then, tell your mother. Tell her.'

Later in the month, Jack was in the living room packing a bag for a freshman orientation day at Bellevue High. It was a Friday morning, three days before the start of the school year. The day was cooler, dry and clear with a touch of autumn. He and Cody were cycling to the high school, and after orientation they were going to Lake Hills Park, where they would use the bike track and visit the rainforest aquarium.

The phone rang. Clare was gardening out back, so he answered it.

'Jack.'

He recognised her voice at once. The musical way she said his name.

'Hi … hi, Carina.'

'I'm happy is you. If your dad answer I don't know what to do.'

Behind her voice was Spanish dance music, not reggaeton but older stuff – salsa or merengue.

'I tried to call you,' he said. 'A few weeks ago. After … you know.'

'I have a new phone.'

He was standing beside the living-room window, looking out at the familiar neighbourhood scene: the mailman's van pulling up to the house across the street, a broken branch lying across the driveway, his bike propped against the trunk of a cottonwood. 'Is everything OK?' he said.

'Yes.'

His shoulders and neck muscles loosened. He had been pressing the receiver tight against his ear.

'How is Feen?' she said.

'He's gone home. To Ireland.'

'*Niño tonto.*'

'*Tonto?*'

'Fool.'

'Yes.'

'And your parents?'

'We made up a story. They don't know.'

The background music filled the silence: brass, drums, maracas. It made Jack think of the corner store in High Point, where they had spent their last few minutes together.

'Ramón, he think police will come. Another *tonto*.'

'Is he bothering you?'

'I no see Ramón anymore. No see that *pandilla*.'

'I was wondering what happened.'

'Is long time ago now. Is different time now.'

'So what are you doing these days?'

'I get ready for school.'

'West Seattle.'

'Westside, yes. The Wildcats. There was family day for freshmen last week. My father take me there.'

'I have orientation today.'

'We have family, you have orientation.'

She laughed, and the laugh helped him picture her face

as it had looked after their kiss: eyes bright, lips moist, skin brown and smooth. *I miss you*, he wanted to say, but for the moment his mouth seemed glued shut.

'I join the band,' she said. 'At school.'

'You play? What do you play?'

'Flute.'

'I didn't know you played the flute.'

'How you know? I never tell you.'

This new detail added mystery. There was so much he didn't know.

'When I was at school,' she said, 'I saw the Wildcats' football schedule. You are the Wolverines, no?'

'Yeah.'

'Our team play yours in October. The first Friday.'

From down the street Cody approached on his bike, standing as he pedalled, his hair riffling in the breeze. Nearing the house he flexed his arms and smoothly jumped the curb.

'Are you going to come to the game?' he said.

Framed by the window, Cody skidded to a stop in the gravel drive. He noticed Jack looking down at him and nodded. Jack waved.

Another laugh, easy and distinct over the brassy music.

'Well,' he said, 'are you?'

'You never know.'